Welcome Home

A Story of Hope, Perseverance, and
Redemption from the Vietnam War

D. Leroy Brown

Published by:

D. Leroy Brown
P.O. Box 66
Strawberry Plains, TN 37871

First Edition © 2024 by D. Leroy Brown

Softcover ISBN: 979-8-218-57699-8

Disclaimer

This book, "Welcome Home," is a work of fiction. Incidents, dialogue, and all characters, with the exception of known historical figures and events, are products of the author's imagination and are not to be construed as real. Welcome Home is not intended to depict actual events. Where real-life historical figures and events appear, the situations, incidents, and dialogues concerning those persons are fictional except for those that are cited and referenced. In all other respects, any resemblance to actual persons, living or dead, events, or locales is entirely coincidental.

All photos by D. Leroy Brown 1970.

Dedication

This book is dedicated to the sailors who served in the
Brown Water Navy during the Vietnam War.

About the Author

D. Leroy Brown is a Navy Vietnam veteran who received the Navy Achievement Award for coastal patrols in the South China Sea and a Navy Commendation with a combat insignia for his service on river patrols in the Mekong Delta in 1970. He lives with his wife of 40 years near his daughter and grandson in eastern Tennessee.

Contents

Abbreviations and Terminology

ATSB. Advanced Tactical Support Base. Relatively crude bases are often found in remote locations.

PBR. A diesel-powered shallow draft gunboat that used Jacuzzi water jets instead of propellers for propulsion. The hull was fiberglass, and the primary armament was .50-caliber machine guns.

STAB. Strike Assault Boat. A fast, four-person gunboat armed with M-60 machine guns and grenade launchers that used gasoline engines and stern drives for propulsion. 20 STABs were sent to Vietnam.

STABRON 20. Strike Assault Boat River Operations Navy, the gunboat squadron made up of 20 STABs.

YRBM. An unpowered barge modified for use as a floating base for Brown Water Navy sailors.

AK-47. The 7.62 mm Avtomat Kalashnikova rifle, designed in the Soviet Union, was the primary rifle used by communist forces during the Vietnam War.

B-40. A rocket-propelled grenade with some armor-piercing capability used throughout the war by the Viet Cong to attack U.S. and South Vietnamese vehicles, boats and bunkers.

M-16. The 5.56 mm caliber rifle used by America forces during the Vietnam War.

M-60. A 7.62 mm machine gun used by U.S. forces.

H&I. Harassment and interdiction fire designed to disrupt or discourage enemy operations in areas where they were expected to assemble or wait in ambush.

ARVN. Army of the Republic of Vietnam, also known as the South Vietnamese Army, who were defeated by the North Vietnamese Army.

CIA. The U.S. Central Intelligence Agency.

CIO. The intelligence agency for the South Vietnam government.

MACV. The U.S. Military Assistance Command, Vietnam formed in February 1962 by the U.S. Army, U.S. Navy, and U.S. Air Force. It included their respective special operations forces. MACV oversaw the U.S. military operations in Vietnam and surrounding areas until the end of March 1973.

DRV. The Democratic Republic of Vietnam was the official name for the government of North Vietnam. After the South's surrender, the entire country of Vietnam was renamed the Socialist Republic of Vietnam.

COSVN. Central Office of Vietnam. Communist party headquarters for South Vietnam.

NVA. The North Vietnamese Army was the army of the DRV.

Viet Minh. The insurgent group was formed by Ho Chí Minh in 1941 to fight the French occupation of Vietnam.

Viet Cong. The term used to describe the Vietnamese communist insurgents, the fighting arm of the National Liberation Front. The term Viet Cong replaced the Viet Minh in the early 1960s.

PRG. The Provisional Revolutionary Government of South Vietnam, the VC's political organization, formed in 1969 as an alternative to South Vietnam's government.

NLF. The National Liberation Front was the formal revolutionary organization formed in 1960 to overthrow the democratic South Vietnamese government.

Khmer Rouge. The communist insurgents operating in Cambodia under the leadership of Pol Pot. They defeated Cambodian forces in 1975 and reigned until their defeat by the Socialist Republic of Vietnam in 1979.

March 1970 — The Awakening

As night fell, Gunner's Mate Josh Harding sat quietly in the Strike Assault Boat 211 nestled in the willows, watching and listening for movement as darkness filled the empty spaces in the jungle. The canal shimmered with the sunset's pink light. Harding's gunboat had set up an ambush east of Phuoc Xuyen, a small village about halfway down the La Grange Canal in the Mekong Delta south of the Cambodian border. Officially known by its English interpretation, the Grand Canal had been renamed The Ditch by sailors of the Brown Water Navy. It was an old rice trade route dug during the French Colonial era to link the Mekong Delta to Saigon.

This was Harding's first week setting up waterborne ambushes in this new four-person gunboat as part of Operation Barrier Reef. In a little-known phase of the Vietnam War, Operation Barrier Reef arrayed a fleet of U.S. Navy gunboats: PBRs, Assault Support Boats, and STABs in a picket line along the canals and rivers opposite the Cambodian border. Infiltration routes and supply lines out of Cambodia fed troops and weapons to the North Vietnamese Army's encirclement strategy of Saigon. This Navy picket line of shallow-water gunboats and helicopter gunships threatened to disrupt the NVA's supply lines and battle plans.

The engineman cupped one last cigarette in his hands before darkness made its glow a target. Enemy agents and scouts, some concealed and some passing by in disguise, attempted to pinpoint the positions of the gunboats whenever the NVA planned a crossing. A troop crossing could not afford to be delayed and risk being gunned down by the Navy's Sea Wolf helicopters or a fixed-wing Black Pony armed with deadly mini-guns.

As night fell over the canal, Harding was looking east when three streaks of light shot across it in the blink of an eye. Turning to the boat captain, he whispered, "I just saw light streak across the canal."

He did not realize he was witnessing a Viet Cong sapper squad ambush a patrol boat from a PBR squadron.

First class petty officer Mark Borders turned up the volume on the radio slightly, which had been turned down to avoid revealing the boat's position. All four of the boat's crew huddled around the speaker.

"We've been hit!" a voice shrieked from the PBR's radio. "KIAs and wounded. Send help." PBRs were diesel-powered, fiberglass-hulled patrol boats with several feet of freeboard that made them a fat target for the Viet Cong's rocket-propelled grenades, also known as B-40s.

Nearby patrol boats responded, but it was too late for two of the crewmen, one of whom was killed instantly. Another bled out in the boat well. The boat captain sustained serious shrapnel wounds to his legs.

The ambush was over in a flash. The Viet Cong squad had accomplished its objective with three B-40s before disappearing into the darkness of the dense jungle. There were no tracer rounds from return fire.

Borders told the engineman, nicknamed Westy, and Harding to get on the M-60 machine guns on either side of the boat cockpit. Harding clicked the safety off on his M-60.

Westy's real name was Westford Hollins. He had this funny shtick of repeating commands from superiors under his breath, followed by a satirical remark and squawk. There was no squawk tonight.

In Harding's boat, alertness turned to fear. It welled up inside the boat crews all along the canal. Borders scanned the opposite bank with a Starlight scope, a night vision device that gave his crew an advantage over the enemy during the dark hours. The night could erupt with another rocket attack at any second. Boat crews felt like sitting ducks — sailors confined to a small boat, hoping to be spared ambush by an enemy creeping through the dark jungle.

As the night wore on, the prospect of another ambush faded. The crew took turns lying on the gun boxes to catch a few winks.

The fear was crippling unless they found some way to deal with it. Unbeknownst to Harding and many combat veterans, it contributed to disorders later that few back home understood. It was worse for those who had to stuff the body parts of their friends into body bags, not knowing which piece of the liver belonged to which KIA. Few escaped the aftermath of mortal combat.

The night's action was not Harding's first hostile fire event. This one did not even score as a combat event on his record. It was hard to pinpoint the first official combat event since there had been a couple of close calls from enemy fire and one thirty-minute firefight, which he was lucky to have survived.

In the meantime, he had to find some way to deal with the fear. Hostile fire events were increasing along the canal, with ambushes once or twice each week. Only 16 PBRs and STABs were on patrol each night on this stretch of the canal, so the chance that his number was going to be called was uncomfortably high. And there were fatalities with every successful ambush.

Most STAB crews started patrolling by training on PBRs, the abbreviation for the diesel-powered Patrol Boat River. Their Strike Assault Boats, STABs for short, were delayed by a mechanical failure on the old landing ship tank transporting the boats across the Pacific. This was the STAB crews' first week on patrol, with ten months to go in the deployment.

Little did Harding know, the attack on this night was part of a North Vietnam Army strategy to grease their infiltration routes across the Mekong Delta with the blood of American sailors.

Enlisting

In the late 1960s, many young men sent to Vietnam were selected based on their economic or academic standing. During the Vietnam War, the military draft, unknown to the coddled youth of future generations, seemed like a death sentence if your number was called. Most men drafted into the military were headed to war in Southeast Asia.

At the height of the war, a young man simply could not opt out of military service unless he acquired a legal status that entitled him to avoid being drafted into the Army. There were workarounds to avoid Army duty. Enlisting in the Navy was one option. The Navy had no problem obtaining recruits, most of whom were escaping the draft and the prospect of crawling around in muddy rice paddies.

For the lucky and well-off, college attendance with a B average exempted them from the draft until they graduated, after which their number went back into the lottery to be drawn randomly. A student who ran out of money or fell from grace academically was snapped up quickly. There were no government-sponsored student loans. Fathers who did not earn enough to pay for college felt immense guilt as their sons headed off to fight a war in an obscure southeast Asian country.

The "domino effect" theory prevailed in the public discourse and was used to justify the sacrifice of America's young men to war. Absent U.S. intervention, communism would spread like cancer throughout Southeast Asia, according to this theory adopted by the political and military elite of the day.

Except most of America's youth were not buying into the domino theory. They joked satirically among themselves that there might be an invasion of Hawaii by a fleet of Viet Cong sampans, underscoring the questionable threat North Vietnam posed to the homeland. On top of that, the enemy had no navy or air force to speak of.

So, some candidates for the draft joined the National Guard, facilitated by politically connected parents. Others got married and had kids. For many, aspiring for IV-F status, which meant they were not medically qualified for any level of military service, was the chosen strategy.

One of Harding's college friends tried to convince everyone that he had a terminal illness, as if his delusional thoughts were enough to keep him from serving. Like if you really aren't terminally ill, just believing you are and making up symptoms will convince a doctor to disqualify you from the draft.

Others, like the rock star Greg Allman, acquired a self-inflicted medical disqualification. Greg shot himself in the foot. Some accepted the consequences of being drafted but, upon being notified, protested by throwing a television out their third-story dorm room window. Fear of the draft hung over an entire generation like a thick, gray fog.

Harding and his college roommate were running out of money and partying their way to a C average. One night, while pondering their fate over a few beers, they made the mistake of venturing down to the theater to watch The Sand Pebbles, a popular Steve McQueen movie. The movie, set in the 1920s, depicted McQueen's heroic character, Jake Holman, on a gunboat fighting the Chinese along the Yangtze River. Their mission was to rescue his love, and a few missionaries caught up in Chiang Kai-shek's fight to unify the country. McQueen's marksmanship in the final scene was excellent for a machinist's mate, who, in the real Navy, rarely touched a gun. They worked on steam engines, not guns.

The next day, without adult supervision or parental consent, which Harding blamed on his roommate, the two floundering students walked into the recruiter's office in the basement of the post office in Knoxville, Tennessee, and joined the Navy.

Enlisting in the Navy was a relief from the fear of the draft. Sailing about the world seemed more illustrious than squirming around in a muddy foxhole or rice paddy in Vietnam, even if it was for four years instead of the two years required by conscription. Little did Harding know at the time, he was destined for combat fighting Asians, like McQueen's character in the movie.

In those days, enlistees could sign their agreement and defer active duty for three months. It was like offering recruits an excuse to goof off and drink beer for three months while awaiting induction to active duty. He spent the time living with a married couple in a muddy trailer park.

Fred had impregnated his girlfriend, so he had to quit school to support his fledgling family. Harding stayed in the trailer during the day, listening to Ray Charles records, drinking beer, and playing his guitar while caring for Fred's pregnant wife, who had trouble maneuvering through the confines of a narrow trailer. Fred made enough money working in a department store to keep them fed.

Finally, the day came for active duty. There was no celebratory farewell dinner. Gripped by a hollow feeling, Harding was dropped off at the processing center in Atlanta by a family friend.

The processing center was an old, abandoned warehouse repurposed for the war. Harding would be there for three nights, getting probed, poked, and screened for induction. At night, giant rats scurried along the baseboards. It was shocking to think that the squeaky-clean United States government was running a rat-infested facility like this. This was just the first of many disillusionments coming his way.

Harding boarded the flight to San Diego for basic training after passing his physical and getting his hair shaved to the scalp.

In the 1960s, basic training was an industrial operation that smashed a recruit's intellectual being into pieces and put it into a mold that served the military's interests, which was all about following orders. Sounds terrible, but no. Many recruits learned discipline they had never known. It served them well in later years, but in the meantime, it was a shock. Some washed out. If you need daily doses of love and affirmation to feel good about yourself, don't go to boot camp.

A few desperate recruits developed strategies to escape basic training. One recruit, who feared losing his girlfriend, in desperation, had her write him a letter claiming that his mother had contracted a terminal illness, which was a lie. Instead of being sent home, he was transferred to the infamous Company 4050, where Military Police ran recruits, convicted in a Captain's Mast, about the base all day, a shovel at port arms with buckets of sand dangling from each elbow joint.

These forlorn recruits were supposed to fill the buckets and run to the other side of the base while under guard. Of course, most wisely collapsed after a few yards to unburden themselves of the sand. As Harding's company marched about doing their drills, the jangles of Company 4050 recruits' buckets clanging on the pavement could be heard across the base, a dire warning to all the recruits within earshot. As they jogged by, bloody bandages dangled from their elbows and knees.

The point of this spectacle was to impress upon recruits that this fate was the consequence of not obeying orders or otherwise complying with the basic training program. It looked like torture. Harding wondered how the Navy could get away with it. Most recruits were sufficiently terrified to double down on their pushups and locker organization without the specter of Company 4050.

Then, one day, Company 4050 disappeared. Scuttlebutt, the Navy term for rumors, claimed that a recruit had written to his family about it, launching a congressional investigation that terminated 4050 and the career of the base commander.

After basic training, Harding went to gunnery school at the Navy's Great Lakes training facility near Chicago before receiving orders to join the crew of a small, wooden minesweeper bound for patrol along the Vietnam coast. The *USS Fortitude*'s 74-man crew could have made up the cast of a situation comedy. The cramped quarters were like living and working in an orange crate.

Sea trials were conducted to test the operational well-being of the Fortitude and the readiness of the crew before the ship began a nine-month cruise to Vietnam by way of Hawaii and the Philippines. The cruise was the adventure Harding was looking forward to. Enroute to Hawaii, the Fortitude spent nearly two weeks wallowing forward in ten-foot seas with two other minesweepers. He never got seasick, but a few were vomiting intermittently throughout the transit to Hawaii.

One young seaman simply could not take it. The captain made him stand watch on the bridge with a bucket even when the dry heaves had him bellowing like a sick cow. His bellows were audible through the sound tube from the bridge to the pilothouse, where Harding steered the ship during his watch duty. After several days, seaman Eastland had seizures brought on by dehydration. He was not faking. When the Fortitude got to Hawaii, he flew back to the States for shore duty.

By the time the Fortitude reached Hawaii, planks that made up the worm-guard had come loose, splaying from the boat's hull like porcupine quills. The ship would be in dry dock for a few days for repairs, while the crew enjoyed a reprieve on liberty in Honolulu.

Then, they returned to sea on a long voyage to the Philippines. The Fortitude's freshwater storage tanks ran dry when at sea for more than a few days. The ship desalinated just enough seawater for one shower every two weeks for lower-ranked enlisted personnel. Even then, the water would only run for a few seconds as crew members learned the meaning of Navy showers.

Upon reaching the tropics, as if on cue, one of the air conditioning compressors failed. The captain's quarters and radio room were stifling hot without the compressor. Captain Cushman opened his port holes for ventilation. The heat from the radio tubes in the radio room made duty there very difficult, so a fan was installed to vent the heat out.

As the Fortitude rocked through the rolling seas, the monotony of the voyage across the international dateline was punctuated by pods of whales breaching and blowing close to the ship. Flying fish sailed from the crest of the foamy waves in a remarkable display of nature's diversity. Some landed on the deck.

One wise guy seaman put a few dead flying fish through the porthole into the captain's stateroom. The next day, the boilermakers moved the only working air conditioning compressor from the crew's berthing quarters to the AC unit that cooled the captain's quarters. They said it was needed there to keep the ship's radios cool.

The captain closed his porthole to prevent more flying fish deposits. His compassion for the crew had not been rewarded. While in the tropics, Harding and many others slept on the deck for days to escape the heat and stench of their berthing quarters.

The berthing compartment consisted of "racks" stacked 28 inches apart, with taut canvas stretched over an aluminum frame covered by a thin mattress. The officers' quarters, on the other hand, seemed palatial, with a freshwater shower, air conditioning, and stewards to serve their meals and keep their uniforms pressed. The "Officer of the Day" in command of the ship on the bridge stood there spouting orders in his ironed khakis while crew members stood watch in rumpled denims that had not been washed for two weeks. The disparity created resentment, particularly among some of the black seamen.

Duty on the *Fortitude* was worthy of toothless buccaneers. Nonetheless, most of the crew had pride in their creaking wooden ship. Sailors performed their duties earnestly, even when the working conditions were not good for their well-being. The cheerful Boatswain's Mate, First Class Petty Officer Martin, who oversaw the deck hands, was the best at personnel management – always looking for ways to slip his men something extra to ease the trials of day after day at sea. After reaching the coast of Vietnam, the Fortitude patrolled the coast every day for two months, stretching the crew and engines to the limit before returning to Subic Bay in the Philippines for repairs.

There were risks on this cruise, depending on your job. After a few years of duty, gunners and enginemen were notoriously hard of hearing, especially after serving in the combat zone. Harding lost much of his high-frequency hearing while at sea along the coast of Vietnam, teaching crew members to shoot a variety of small arms off the fantail as part of Sunday recreation and training. He stood to the left to avoid the shell casings ejecting from the right side of the weapon. He shot 50-caliber machine guns and twin 20 mm cannons in live fire exercises as the ship prepared for the combat zone. It was recreation for everyone but him, since long shooting sessions left him with ringing ears and a pile of automatic weapons to clean.

The corpsman on the Fortitude claimed he was out of earplugs after Harding lost his. "Doc" had been reprimanded for being out of position during a steering casualty. He was "grab-assing" with the engineman during underway replenishment when the ship veered off to starboard, snapping a two-inch manila highline and dumping a pallet of stores into the South China Sea. The engineman, who controlled the pitch of the two screws to set the vessel's speed, was having trouble matching the speed of the supply ship while Doc harassed him. At some point, the starboard screw reversed pitch, forcing the ship to starboard.

Doc blamed Harding for his record getting dinged after the investigation. As a result, he would not make Chief Petty Officer. He retaliated by withholding earplugs when Harding needed replacements. Harding went through seven months of live fire exercises and target practice on the Fortitude without earplugs. The raging headaches and ringing in his ears lasted for two hours after each day of shooting drills.

The Fortitude spent most of the nine months in the western Pacific, five of them in the combat zone along the Vietnam coast, boarding sampans and light junks looking for enemy weapon shipments. Arms had been smuggled by sea during the early part of the war, but Navy coastal patrols had shut down most coastal smugglers.

As the only gunner on this small ship, Harding's job was to jump from the fantail onto a sampan or junk summoned alongside for inspection as it heaved in the swells. He wiggled into the hold, usually filled with fishing nets, to look for weapons. The flak jacket, boots, and 45 caliber pistol strapped across his chest assured that the bottom of the South China Sea was his next stop if he missed the landing on the sampan.

No weapons were ever found, but this taste of the war, the lure of combat pay, and the squalid living conditions on the Fortitude prompted him to volunteer for the Brown Water Navy, the illustriously reckless gunboat crews fighting the Viet Cong on the rivers and canals in the Mekong Delta.

While Harding's request for transfer to the Brown Water Navy was processed, the little wooden minesweeper bobbed its way back to Long Beach, towing another disabled minesweeper for most of the 3,000 miles across the Pacific. It took 30 days to reach Long Beach from Sasebo, Japan. To Harding, Long Beach seemed like the armpit of the world. It was hopelessly devoid of worthwhile feminine companionship, priority number one for twenty-year-olds. He had to get out.

Orders

Harding's escape from the Fortitude and Long Beach was realized when he received orders to train with the Brown Water Navy's new Strike Assault Boat Squadron River Operations Navy, STABRON 20 for short. The squadron was headed to Vietnam at the end of 1969. The low profile, 24-foot-long STAB was powered by two 325 horsepower, 427 cubic inch gasoline engines. Self-sealing aircraft fuel bladders kept the thirsty engines running for hours. Light armor and flak curtains surrounded the four-person boat well. STABs were fast and quiet compared to the diesel-powered PBRs. They were designed for quick strikes, but their high-performance engines presented a logistical challenge. Good gasoline for high-performance engines was not readily available in Vietnam's boondocks, so a gasoline barge had to be towed and anchored wherever the boats were based.

Strike Assault Boat 1970, Ben Thuy, South Vietnam.

STAB crews spent two months training in Vallejo, California's reedy marshes, learning to operate the new boats. Training wrapped up with survival school in Whidbey Island, where sailors who were headed for combat learned to survive if missing in action or taken prisoner.

There was no food for the entire week. The end of the fourth day was spent evading capture while orienteering through the woods to a rendezvous point, only to end with internment in a mock prisoner-of-war camp. The menacing staff wore communist uniforms with one red star on their specially styled commie caps.

The Commandant of the camp was a *USS Pueblo* survivor who spent 11 months in North Korean POW camps after the ship's capture in the infamous 1968 incident. The Pueblo was a lightly armed vessel conducting electronic intercepts of North Vietnamese communications when it was captured in international waters 16 miles off the North Korean coast.

The Commandant knew how to run a mock POW camp. After capture during internment and orientation, new POWs crawled naked on their hands and knees through a gauntlet while the camp's staff made fun of their genitals. "Look at that tiny weenie!" and stuff like that. STAB crews spent three sleepless nights in a muddy compound cordoned by razor wire. To ensure they got no sleep, air raid sirens went off every 20 minutes, requiring muster in the compound. There was no food and little water.

Everyone went through an interrogation. The interrogators singled out the weak by offering them early release to sign documents admitting to atrocities and verifying fictitious charges against their comrades. The interrogator told Harding that a prisoner had ratted on another prisoner and asked him for confirmation, which was the first big mistake one could make.

Harding knew to resist. The naïve souls who fell for it were unraveled shortly thereafter. For punishment, they were partially submerged in the cold water contained in two 55-gallon drums welded together and buried in the ground at a 45-degree angle, all while being asked for additional fabricated admissions to escape punishment. Some were brushed about the neck with a stinging nettle close enough to the compound to be visible to all the POWs. No one was ever permanently injured, but the lessons were indelible.

The guards also knew how to shock with physical intimidation. If you resisted their orders to get in line, they whacked you hard on your cheekbone with the heel of their hand. It was unexpected and stunning to be hit so hard as part of training.

Harding's interrogator attempted to rough him up after he failed to comply during the interrogation. He shocked the interrogator with wrestling skills developed in high school, throwing him against the wall in a heap. The camp guard was stunned and emerged from his role briefly to advise Harding not to do that again, as if he was really going to get in trouble. Then he meekly returned to his desk and dismissed Harding as quickly as possible, fearing another eruption.

In a real POW camp, Harding would have been tortured into submission. This fake camp was just a game, and Harding knew it.

After returning to the compound, Harding planned an escape by getting a group to distract the guard in the tower and creating a ruckus on one side of the compound while he shimmied under the razor wire on his back. It worked, and he hung out in the woods for a while before reporting to the camp command. Hanging out in the compound was much better than being alone in the dark, cold woods of Washington state at night. The reward for escaping was a cup of coffee and an apple while sitting in a warm, dry building for a few minutes before returning to the wet, muddy compound.

The fading light of sunset was the only indication of time since all their watches had been taken at the start of the week. When it was near the time for the prisoners' internment to end, guards brought in a big iron pot of beef roast, cabbage, carrots, and onions and set it aboil on the camp's fire. The forlorn POWs were sure the excruciating ordeal was over as the wonderful smell of cooking food wafted from the pot.

Just before it was done, the guards came in yelling that they had learned of Harding's escape, and because other prisoners had collaborated, they were not getting to eat. The guards kicked the pot over, and the wonderful steaming food settled into the mud as they left the compound, laughing.

Everyone looked at Harding. Some with disgust, but most knew it was a ruse. Time drug on for another night in captivity. At daybreak, the guards opened the gates and called an end to the week of survival training. They congratulated the prisoners for getting through it and laughed while reciting several events that entertained them during the week.

The Whidbey Island prison camp was a taste of the psychological destitution inflicted upon POWs without the physical torture accompanying the real thing. The STAB crews flew back to Vallejo in an old DC-3, ready for deployment to South Vietnam. They were scheduled to fly to Saigon from San Francisco just before midnight on Christmas Eve.

The night before departure, Boatswain's Mate Jack Goodings invited Harding to join him and a couple of others on liberty in San Francisco. They rambled around the city before landing at Rosie O'Grady's for beer and pizza. Tables were arranged in long lines, as expected, in a beer hall. Shortly after Harding's group was seated, two couples joined them at their long table.

Harding introduced himself to break the ice and said, "This is Jack, George, and Westy." The two couples looked to be in their thirties and responded with their names. But their leader, Brian, was eyeing Harding's crew curiously. Harding knew something wasn't right when they started conversing under their breath.

The waiter took their order.

Then Brian asked the sailors if they were in the military, which was obvious from their haircuts. Jack said, "Navy. We are headed to Vietnam tomorrow."

Brian stood up and summoned the group to move to another table. As they were sitting down, Jack said, "Hey dude!" and flipped them off. Brian stood up angrily and waved to the others to follow as he headed for the door. "Don't kill any babies!" he said indignantly.

A few minutes later, the waiter arrived, perplexed to find them gone. Goodings explained the circumstances, and the waiter gave the STAB sailors their beer at no charge. They had won their first hostile action of the war.

Entertainment at Rosie's was a Dixieland band with a banjo and horns playing old standards while the words to the songs flashed on a screen in the background. It was campy and corny in the days of Jefferson Airplane and hip British rock bands, but Harding and his buddies drank beer and sang all night. It would be their last party for a while.

The somber STAB squadron boarded a Flying Tiger Airlines' DC-8 bound for Saigon just before midnight on December 24th. No one was talking in part because most just wanted to sleep. Ironically, "Leaving on a Jet Plane" was playing on someone's transistor radio as they boarded the bus for the airport. The DC-8 flew north to refuel in Anchorage before the long flight to Japan for the last leg to Saigon. By the time they landed in sunny Tan Son Nhut, it was December 26th of their year without Christmas.

Cambodia, December 1969

The Pilatus PC Porter landed on the short dirt strip on the outskirts of Phnom Penh. CIA agent Homer Gentry hopped off the short takeoff and landing aircraft owned by Air America, the CIA-owned airline flying throughout Southeast Asia, to support the war effort. He walked toward the Cambodian officer, who was awaiting his arrival.

Colonel Kou was the Deputy Chief of Staff for the Cambodian Minister of Defense, Lon Nol. The meeting with a lower-ranking officer diminished its profile. Colonel Kou was less likely to be tracked by President Sihanouk's agents.

Kou was secretly serving the interests of Prince Matak. He hoped to gain favor with the Prince by assisting with his efforts to stage a coup against Sihanouk.

The CIA knew that the forever vain Prince Norodom Sihanouk was expected to leave the country at the end of February for his annual visit to a weight-loss spa in the south of France. It was the CIA's opportunity to promote change to a regime aligned with U.S. interests.

Sihanouk's departure convened with the unease building within the leadership of the Cambodian military over the NVA annexation of the three eastern Cambodian provinces for use as weapon depots and gateways for their infiltration into South Vietnam.

Cambodian military leaders were concerned that the NVA might support communist Pol Pot's Khmer Rouge and their efforts to make Cambodia a communist state. But Sihanouk's tacit alliance with Russia and China had stalled North Vietnam's support for Pol Pot's insurgency.

Sihanouk, while feigning neutrality, had allied himself with North Vietnam and the Soviet block by allowing weapons shipments to be transferred to the NVA through the port of Sihanoukville. The Russians and Chinese bankrolled Sihanouk with financial assistance in return for the use of Cambodia's ports and provinces.

Prince Matak and Lon Nol were frustrated that Prince Sihanouk did not see the danger unfolding along the border with his double-dealing. The prospect of Cambodia once again being controlled by Vietnam, their historic enemies, could not be tolerated.

Gentry's visit was another secret mission that would never be attributable to any official U.S. government agency. Gentry had decided to take action on his own after a quiet conversation with commanders in Saigon. Since the U.S. could not convince Prince Sihanouk to shut down the port of Sihanoukville to arms shipments through official channels, the CIA's initiative to quietly support a coup was the last option.

Intelligence reports estimated that "between December 1966 and April 1969, Chinese vessels had delivered at least 21,600 tons of military and 5,300 tons of nonmilitary cargo to Sihanoukville, Cambodia's only seaport for dry cargo. From there, it went by truck convoy to North Vietnamese depots on the border."[1]

A small industry had grown up among Cambodians, delivering weapons from Sihanoukville to NVA border sanctuaries. Meanwhile, NVA troops were flowing down the Ho Chí Minh Trail from the north to rendezvous with the weapons arriving in the Cambodian port.

By 1969, Cambodian border provinces were major staging areas for NVA troops before crossing into South Vietnam. Roads supported truck traffic through Laos, but most of the weapons went to the northernmost provinces of South Vietnam. Sihanoukville supplied weapons to the communists in the Delta region, and the U.S. desperately wanted it shut down before handing the war off to the South Vietnamese military.

Finally, as the quest to end the war consumed Washington politicians, Sihanouk's alliance with the communists tipped their hand and sealed his fate. President Nixon had already authorized the secret bombing of staging areas in Cambodia. The generals in the U.S. desperately wanted to conduct ground operations in Cambodia, but Sihanouk objected and threatened to abandon his lame neutrality, so the Pentagon nixed those operations for the time being. Protests against the escalation of the war were also building, so Defense Secretary Laird opposed any escalation for fear it would jeopardize political support for his war effort.

---

[1] *MACV: The Years of Withdrawal, 1968–1973, pg 303.*

Before acting against Sihanouk, Nol and Prince Matak wanted assurances from the U.S. that military aid would flow if they challenged Sihanouk's leadership. Gentry's visit intended to give the coup against Sihanouk an unofficial green light.

Kou approached Gentry and shook his hand. He gestured for Gentry to join him in the backseat of a Chevrolet station wagon provided to the Cambodians, ironically, by the CIA. Gentry refused to get in the car, fearing he would be taped.

It was a dark operation that could cost Gentry his career if it went wrong. But he was a protégé of the famed CIA agent, Edward Lansdale and knew agents sometimes had to stray outside official lines to get things done.

Ironically, the CIA had recruited Cambodian Army Colonel Kou as an asset in 1967, providing him supplemental income for substantive information on Cambodian political and military matters. After greeting Kou, Gentry took him by the arm and walked him closer to Pilatus' idling engine so their conversation could not be overheard.

"I want to offer you my personal advice regarding General Nol and Sihanouk," he told Kou. "While I cannot personally make any promises on behalf of the United States, I think you know that the U.S. cannot allow Cambodia to fall into the wrong hands. Now, Prince Sihanouk has allowed the Viet Cong to open an embassy in Phnom Penh. I believe you can count on U.S. and South Vietnam military support following the successful transition of power to General Nol. The U.S. will not participate directly in the transition, but it is my personal opinion that you will get much support to defeat the NVA and Khmer Rouge when that happens."

"Will you promise weapons and financial support to fight the Khmer Rouge and NVA?" Kou insisted.

"Trust me, if you shut down Sihanoukville to arms shipments and cooperate in other ways, good things will happen. That is my opinion. There are weapons caches hidden in NVA sanctuaries that must go somewhere," implying without commitment that those arms would also be transferred to Nol's forces.

Although Gentry never claimed to be speaking on behalf of the U.S. government, Kou assumed otherwise. Gentry saluted Kou and said, "Good day, Colonel," and hopped back into the Pilatus. The meeting was over in five minutes. The Pilatus taxied to the end of the runway and roared into the cumulus clouds, floating like galleons across the afternoon sky.

Song Ong Doc

Shortly after arriving in Saigon, the STAB squadron spent a few days in orientation at "The Annapolis," slang for the Navy barracks in downtown Saigon. The curriculum included lessons in Vietnamese culture, phrase books, and customs. The instructor said Vietnamese men liked to hold hands with their friends when they talked, so sailors should not be freaked out. Relax and go with it. Everyone laughed.

While the STAB squadron settled in at the Annapolis, their boats were still making their way across the Pacific on an old LST. After a few days in Saigon, Harding and other STAB sailors flew by helicopter to the USS Benewah, a barracks ship originally commissioned at the end of World War II and brought out of mothballs to serve as a floating base for the Brown Water Navy operations during the Vietnam war. Anchored in the Mekong a few miles downstream of the Cambodian border, the Benewah served as a base of operation for the Navy's patrol boats.

The flight over the delta to the Benewah in an old Korean War era, "Jolly Green," was enlightening. The old copter vibrated like a paint can shaker. Harding thought this vibrating jalopy had to be experiencing metal fatigue. It could fall out of the sky at any moment. A couple of months later, one did. Harding's letter to his parents, along with other outbound mail, was returned to the authors stained with blood after the Jolly Green had crashed. The Navy did not want families back home receiving blood-stained mail.

Flying over Vietnam's landscape, Harding thought about how it resembled a landscape with acne. Portions of it were scarred with bomb craters, sometimes in clusters and, in other places, with big, individual craters.

Two days after arriving on the Benewah, Petty Officer Johnson and Harding flew by helicopter to a Tactical Support Base at the mouth of the Song Ong Doc River bordering the infamous U Minh Forest, a Viet Cong stronghold. Their temporary duty and mission at Song Ong Doc: planting Sonobuoy sensors in the trees in the

23

U Minh and marking their coordinates so the ARVN could drop 105 mm rounds on their location when the sensor broadcast the sound of Viet Cong movements. These were disposable sensors designed for antisubmarine warfare modified for this terrestrial operation. The sensors turned on at night and broadcast audio back to a bunker, where U.S. and Vietnamese sailors sat listening for hours to jungle noises through headphones. A perimeter of Sonobuoys was supposed to constitute a defense perimeter for a vulnerable base. Only once in four weeks did they detect anything remotely sounding like the enemy.

This electronic surveillance operation was dubbed Operation Duffle Bag by the Navy. Navy contractors thought this to be remarkably clever technology in convincing the Pentagon to adopt it, but the VC were one step ahead of them. The enemy's local intelligence network always seemed to know where the sensors were.

The U Minh was infested with VC. The VC were kept at bay by the dribble of money from the little Navy outpost at the mouth of the river and the medical care the corpsmen and doctors donated to the locals and their children. Their mothers kept the VC from attacking the base for a while. But it was a wild, edgy place, one that could be wiped out any day by enemy mortars.

Harding lived in a tent with Vietnamese sailors assigned to this joint operation during this temporary duty. Their compound was inside a lightly guarded perimeter and was not part of the floating barges at the mouth of the river that made up the base for the Seal Team and gunboat crews.

Duffle Bag sailors spent the days lollygagging around, cleaning weapons, and snoozing. They sat in a bunker on four-hour shifts at night, listening to the Sonobuoys broadcast sounds from the nearby swamp.

The Song Ong Doc deployment delivered the first installment of events leading to Harding's disillusionment with the Vietnam War effort. The Vietnamese sailors assigned to the Duffle Bag operation were of Chinese descent from the Cholon District in Saigon. Chinese were not highly regarded in Vietnam, as they later explained. They said they were treated like blacks in America. China invaded and occupied Vietnam for long periods centuries ago. The latest occupation was in the 15th century. The Vietnamese have long memories.

Friction between the Vietnamese and one of the U.S. sailors from California boiled over one day. He argued with the Vietnamese over their lack of commitment to winning the war. Blows were exchanged after he called them "gooks." He was transferred out of Song Ong Doc the next day, which was fine with Harding because he was not a pleasant fellow.

Harding apologized to the Vietnamese for his remarks, and they became friends. They confided to him that the dispute erupted after they admitted they did not care who won the war. Vietnam had been at war for 20 years. They said the U.S. presence in Vietnam was destroying their country and making whores of their women.

Harding did not know if this opinion was common among the Vietnamese military, but he was shocked. "How can we help these people win the war if they don't care who wins?" It occurred to him that these "allies" might flip their allegiance in the blink of an eye if the South lost momentum in the war effort.

The Vietnamese in Song Ong Doc were intelligent and affable. They spoke English, Chinese, and Vietnamese and were studying Japanese during their off hours, which was not indicative of most of the poor Vietnamese in the delta.

Song Ong Doc was a treacherous assignment, as Harding discovered shortly after arriving. He noticed one of the Navy Seals fiberglassing a sampan on a stand near his tent. He was converting it into a sailboat. The sail arrived in shipping one day, and the Seal set off into the bay the next day. He never returned. Seals don't drown like that. The VC got him. Letting your guard down could be fatal. An event the next week revealed that VC spies were watching their every move.

Early one afternoon, Harding heard a gunshot and rushed out of his tent with an M-16. A Vietnamese intelligence officer stood over a lifeless body. He had shot a Vietnamese worker who was bringing a grenade onto the base to either frag the Seal Team or set a booby trap. The U.S. hired a few Vietnamese workers as housekeepers. They were supposed to be vetted by Vietnamese intelligence.

Perhaps even more disconcerting was seeing his first Viet Cong prisoner. The mess hall at Song Ong Doc was on one of the barges anchored in the mouth of the river. One day at lunch, Harding noticed this wiry, wild-looking guy in a loincloth squatting on the bench instead of sitting on it. The prisoner, whom the Seals had captured, was guarded by a sailor a few feet away with his hand on a 45. Harding compared this dude to his congenial Vietnamese friends and just shook his head. The Vietnamese seemed so outmatched by this savage-looking guerilla.

On another day, the Duffle Bag sailors were hanging out in their tents before the day's heat made them unbearable. Suddenly, projectiles whistled into the perimeter, followed by explosions and shock waves. They scrambled into the bunker, thinking this was a VC attack on the base.

Instead, it was friendly fire from a U.S. Navy destroyer off the coast, which had been firing rocket-assisted, 5-inch projectiles deep into the U Minh. On this day, for some reason, the rounds fell short into the compound. Fortunately, no one was hurt, but the action taught another lesson about war. In the combat zone, you could just as easily die by the hand of your friend as the hand of your enemy.

And it was sometimes hard to know who the enemy was, as Harding's last mission to plant sensors in the U Minh revealed. Lieutenant Hagerty hired three sampans from the local militia, known as the Ruff Puffs, to carry four sailors and a sensor deep into the U Minh. It was a ragtag group.

"Where was the Seal Team?" Harding wondered. These motley militiamen were on the far end of the military spectrum for what seemed like a very risky mission. Little did he know they were his insurance policy against a VC attack.

Lt. Hagerty ordered Harding to carry the M-60 machine gun in the lead sampan on this mission and to be prepared to lay down fire on command. "Harassment and interdiction" fire involved shooting preemptively in the event the enemy was waiting in the bushes for an ambush.

With the M-60 hanging from a shoulder strap and ammo belts wrapped across his shoulders, Harding almost capsized the narrow sampan as he stepped into it. One untoward lean with heavy bandoleers of machine gun rounds was all it would take to sink this unstable vessel.

Powered by Briggs and Stratton lawnmower motors, the three narrow craft puttered up the main channel of the river before turning into a tributary about 200 yards from the base. The Vietnamese immediately started jabbering "VC, VC, VC," pointing upstream. Harding clicked off the safety, but no one was in sight. After a few more putts from the Briggs and Stratton motor, the Ruff Puffs pointed to keel marks in the mud where two sampans had been hauled from the creek onto the bank and slid into the forest. These Vietnamese escorts seemed to know where these tracks were even before they got there.

The sampans took another turn into a narrow canal no wider than the width of two or three sampans. The brush closed in, making it impossible to see anything off the canal. Lt. Hagerty ordered Harding to lay down H&I fire by sweeping the thickets with 7.62 mm rounds. There was no return fire. Finally, the swamp opened into a forest with large trees and a fan of waterways too sinuous and small for the sampans.

The sampans stopped at a location Lt. Hagerty had pinpointed on his map and noted the coordinates. Harding was ordered to hang a sensor high in one of the trees near the stream. He gave Lt. Hagerty his M-60 to mind while he climbed the tree.

Harding was tying the sensor to the tree branches 45 feet off the ground when explosions erupted from behind his back. "It's over," he thought calmly, "but I'll take a few potshots at them with my 45." These thoughts ran through his head in milliseconds. Remarkably, there was no panic, just a quick resignation that he was about to be shot out of the tree. Then, another explosion followed by excited jabbering in Vietnamese as he turned to see splashing, accompanied by a cacophony of excited Vietnamese exclamations. The Ruff Puffs were stunning catfish with hand grenades and diving in after the floundering fish.

The sampans and their motley crew puttered back to the base without incident. At dusk, when the Sonobuoy turned on, it broadcast an unusual sound back to the Duffle Bagger's bunker. The Vietnamese sailors came running in to tell Harding about the strange sounds they heard through the headphones.

Then, the light bulb moment. It was the sound of a sampan motor. The VC had gotten the sensor. It was being taken back to their base of operation by sampan.

Maybe the catfishing operation was their signal, and the VC watched while Harding hung it in the tree. Or the Ruff Puffs were infiltrated and gave away their position. Harding wondered if they might have even been the ones who got it. Along with their prescient citing of the sampan keel marks, one had to be completely naïve not to suspect them, and it's probably why there was little chance of getting attacked during the operation.

A few days later, Lt. Hagerty sent a message to Harding to meet him in the mess hall. Seal Team leader Bader was with Hagerty. Bader asked Harding if he would man the M-60 on his Boston Whaler during a reconnaissance mission into the

U Minh. Harding was honored to have been asked and accepted the offer but wondered quietly why a Seal Team member wasn't doing it.

The Whaler was powered by an outboard, which seemed incredibly loud for a lightly armed recon mission. The M-60 mount was positioned on a center mount. Harding hung onto the gun as the whaler wound up the remote, uninhabited waterways off the main river. Bader was obviously looking for something. After they turned off the main channel into the canals, it dawned on Harding why no one else wanted to accompany Bader. Two sailors running a noisy outboard deep into enemy territory was not exactly the stealthy operation Seals were trained for. It was high risk.

After half an hour, Bader pulled the boat up to the shore. Harding tied it up to a mangrove branch. Just off the canal, a triangular mud platform about two feet above the high tide spread out before them. Each side was about 60 feet long. A shallow bunker was dug out in the middle, probably for bathing. There were no prints in the damp, elevated ground, which was drier than the mud that surrounded it. This was how the VC survived in the muddy swamps of the U Minh. It was a base for a VC squad, but it did not look like it had been used for a while. There were no shelters, and no trace of trash could be found. Bader and Harding returned to the base at Song Ong Doc without incident.

This was Harding's last mission at Song Ong Doc before returning to the Benewah. Nine months later, the little base at Song Ong Doc was wiped out by 90 mortar and recoilless rifle rounds.

Operation Barrier Reef, Mekong Delta, February 1970

The *USS Benewah* was anchored in the Mekong a few miles from the Cambodian border. The STAB boats had finally reached Vietnam but were being set up in Ben Thuy. In the meantime, STAB crews used the time to train on patrol with PBR squadrons.

Navy operations to disrupt infiltration routes into the Mekong Delta had begun as the U.S. involvement in the war increased, and North Vietnam began moving weapons and troops into the delta through neighboring Cambodia. In 1964, Captain Phillip Bucklew and eight other naval officers were ordered by Admiral Felt, Commander of the Navy's Pacific fleet, to study the infiltration routes into the South.

Admiral Felt told Bucklew, "In a nutshell, I want to know why all I get from Vietnam are glowing reports of our accomplishments, and meanwhile, we are getting the hell kicked out of us. That's your job."[2]

In 1965, the Army found a camouflaged ship full of weapons at Vung Ro Bay along the South Vietnamese coast. The Navy responded with Operation Market Time, a naval blockade of the entire South Vietnamese coast using destroyers, minesweepers, swift boats, and Coast Guard cutters. Harding's first visit to Vietnam on the Fortitude had been part of this operation. By 1969, Operation Market Time had shut down the sea-based smugglers, forcing the North Vietnamese Army to focus its infiltration and supply on inland routes[3].

---

[2] EUGENE F. PALUSO, Lt. Commander, United States Navy Operation Sea Lords: A STUDY IN THE EFFECTIVENESS OF THE ALLIED NAVAL CAMPAIGN OF INTERDICTION (submitted a partial fulfillment for completion of studies for Master's Degree in Military Studies), 2001, page 8.
[3] The Cambodian Incursion, Brigadier General Tran Dinh Tho, ARVN, Maclean, VA, 1978, page 22.

Bucklew's study also found that the North Vietnamese Army and Viet Cong dominated the river systems of the Mekong Delta, using rivers, small streams, and canals to move troops and weapons out of Cambodia. Trawlers full of weapons from Eastern Bloc countries were entering Cambodia through its southern port at Sihanoukville. The South Vietnamese Navy could not stop these waterborne supply lines, especially those along the rivers and canals. But neither could the U.S. Navy.

In 1966, the U.S. Navy launched the Brown Water Navy, slang for the Mobile Riverine Force, consisting of 258 craft, mostly shallow draft gunboats, and 25 helicopter gunships for air support in an operation to disrupt enemy logistics on inland waterways.[4]

It was a rapidly conceived concoction of boats powered by diesel engines, armed with 50-caliber machine guns and, in some cases, heavier weapons. Shallow draft landing craft were converted into heavily armed, armored weapons platforms with 20 mm aircraft cannons. One floating contraption was a single turret, flame-throwing monitor that looked like something out of the Civil War. It was only slightly faster than the steamboats of that era.

The workhorse of the Brown Water Navy was the faster PBR with its fiberglass hull and Jacuzzi water pumps instead of propellers for propulsion. The pumps and hull design allowed the PBRs to operate in a foot of water.

Admiral Elmo Zumwalt took command of naval forces in Vietnam in September 1968 and quickly changed focus to the Mekong Delta infiltration routes. Intelligence reports claimed the 200 tons of weapons and supplies from Eastern Bloc nations entering Cambodia through the port in Sihanoukville were being transported overland to staging areas along the Cambodian border with Vietnam. From there, NVA troops, with assistance from the Viet Cong and an army of clandestine porters, transported weapons by foot or in sampans to bases dispersed throughout the Delta.[5]

The Navy conceived four barrier operations in 1968 to shut down these supply lines. Two of them focused on infiltration routes out of Cambodia. Operation Giant Slingshot began in December 1968 along the Vam Co Tay and Vam Co Dong Rivers, which made up the boundaries of the Parrot's Beak, a protrusion of Cambodian territory thrusting toward Cu Chí and Saigon to the Southeast.

---

[4] Ibid, page 14.
[5] Ibid page 24.

Operation Giant Slingshot was the Navy's deadliest operation, with over 358 sailors killed or wounded during its tenure. Operation Barrier Reef, which had nothing to do with coral, began operation in January 1969 to interdict the flow of weapons and troops from the Cambodian border along the Mekong River and across the Plain of Reeds.

After returning from Song Ong, Doc Harding trained with PBR crews patrolling at night along the Grand Canal. On his second patrol, Boat Captain Dyson ordered him to set up a machine gun position with a Marine sniper on the "beach" over an elevated road in a section of the Canal that cut through the Plain of Reeds. There was no beach in the Plain of Reeds. "Beach" was Navy slang for any ground off the boat. While this assignment on "the beach" had higher risks, to Harding, it was much better than sitting on a boat all night like a sitting duck trying to stay awake and alert.

Much of the verdant plain was converted to rice patties during the French Colonial era. In 1970, fields of reeds that looked like saw grass still covered portions of the plain, providing concealment for the enemy's movements. The cover was just high enough to hide a company of enemy soldiers. The plain was only two feet above sea level, so it flooded during the wet season. The VC used sampans to transport weapons. But this was a drought year, so much of the plain was dry.

The boat captain sent two crew members over the road on an all-night watch to protect the boat and crew. Two sailors alone, out of sight of the boat with a portable radio, M-60 machine gun, M-16s, and grenade launcher, were supposed to protect the boat from ambush by an enemy platoon. It was a dicey proposition, except this guard post was blessed to have a Marine sniper on board.

"Barney" was a good-natured Mexican American whose real name was Angel Estrada. He had assumed the nickname Barney after his drill sergeant in boot camp made fun of having an "angel" in the company. A drill sergeant's mission was to break down any self-esteem recruits had arrived with and replace it with obedience and obsequiousness to their commanders. Berating boot camp recruits was part of the process.

During muster, Sergeant Washington, an 18-year career African-American Marine, got in Angel's face and said loudly, "Are you the company's little angel?"

Estrada said, "No sir. Just call me Barney." It was all he could think of to escape the drill sergeant's wrath.

Sergeant Washington cracked up, quickly catching the reference to Barney Fife of the Andy Griffith Show. He chuckled, which gave the other Marines the impression that it was okay to laugh. When Sergeant Washington heard a few chuckles from the recruits in formation, he gathered himself.

"Who gave you permission to laugh? Are you laughing at me, you worms? Get down and give me elbows and toes," an excruciating exercise that stressed the stomach muscles and pained the elbow joints. Fortunately, they were on a grass drill field and not on asphalt. After a few minutes, all the recruits had collapsed and were required to repent with pushups.

Ironically, Sergeant Washington favored Angel from then on. After he performed at the marksman level in basic training, Sergeant Washington recommended him for sniper school. But Angel realized he might not have the best name for a tough Marine sniper. When he joined the PBR squadron on a temporary assignment, Angel introduced himself as "Barney," as he had done in all his previous assignments. The Navy was famous for irreverent and politically incorrect nicknames. Barney fit right in.

The boat crews loved Barney. Marine snipers had a mixed reception in Vietnam, but in the open spaces of the Plains of Reeds, their presence was welcomed. Barney rotated among boat crews for a few weeks, depending on where intelligence predicted action. Everyone wanted him on their boat to the point of near worship.

Barney only had a few more nights on the canal before his tour ended. Snipers were banished along with napalm and tear gas as politicians took control of the U.S. war effort. Napalm, tear gas and snipers were considered inhumane. Without tear gas, U.S. forces had no way to restrain or deter enemy suspects, so they had to shoot them if under an imminent threat.

Meanwhile, the Viet Cong and NVA continued fighting with any lethal method at their disposal.

Estrada saved their lives on this night on the Plain of Reeds. An hour after nightfall, peering through the Starlight scope mounted on his M14 rifle, he spotted a VC platoon moving toward them in the grass.

As the VC squad approached their position, Harding wondered how they had pinpointed them on this vast plain. Barney radioed the boat captain, who had to radio Winepress, the call sign for their combat command center, to get permission to open fire. This bureaucratic process was another politically correct procedure that evolved after the Mi Lai massacre and negative publicity about civilian casualties. If the VC shot first or a boat crew was in imminent danger, they could shoot without asking for permission, but otherwise, they were supposed to get permission to open fire to avoid collateral damage to "friendlies."

This sanitization of war protocols amused the Viet Cong since it gave them license to hide away among civilians to avoid getting shot.

Fortunately, this enemy squad was emerging from an unpopulated area. With permission to open fire, Barney waited cool as a cucumber as the VC platoon moved into range. They looked like sticks to Harding through the glimmer of the Starlight scope.

Barney had been involved in many combat events, so he didn't let them get too close, nailing the first enemy at 150 yards. Harding naively wanted them closer so he could teach them a lesson with the M-60. Barney fired his rifle repeatedly while Harding raked the dark landscape with the M-60. The likelihood that he hit anyone after Barney's first shot was minimal.

Ten minutes into the firefight, a few rounds were still zinging by their open position. Harding's M-60 jammed. The barrel was glowing red hot. He ripped off his shirt and used it to insulate his hand while removing the barrel. A spent shell casing was stuck in the chamber, which he extracted with the point of another bullet.

Harding was shooting in the dark in the general direction of the VC's last known position. The incoming rounds faded away. The PBR boat captain called for an air strike. Harding and his fellow sailors returned to the PBR to avoid the pending airstrike. After a few minutes, a Seawolf arrived, released flares and began plowing up the landscape with two pods of Zuni rockets and thousands of rounds of 7.62 through its mini-guns.

The VC ran back to the tree line and dispersed when they heard the chopper approaching. The fireworks show was great, nonetheless.

After an hour, the South Vietnamese Army (ARVN) showed up to conduct a sweep. Harding was ordered to lay down H&I fire until the South Vietnamese could start their sweep. Exhibiting undaunted courage, the ARVN forces assembled slowly, ensuring the VCs' retreat was complete, before venturing about 200 yards from the road.

The PBR crew conducted reconnaissance the next morning to look for blood trails but found only one bandage, which curiously had U.S. markings on it. That perplexed Harding until he realized a few months later that the weapons supplied by the United States to some local militias were being given to the Viet Cong. The communists owned the Mekong Delta backcountry, largely unoccupied by U.S. ground forces.

Later, the official report on this firefight said the PBR crew and airstrikes had killed 19 enemy combatants, a lie that was another installment in the propaganda campaign designed to make parents feel better about the sacrifice of their children to the war effort. Barney had mortally wounded at least one Viet Cong fighter, but the military brass had inflated the casualty count way beyond that. It was a rude awakening for Harding. Navy brass appeared to be padding enemy casualty counts to advance their careers.

Even so, Navy gunboats were disrupting the NVA's invasion of South Vietnam through the Mekong Delta. After successful daylight interdictions, the enemy resorted to nighttime movements through open terrain when they were harder to detect. By 1970, in the Mekong Delta, the ground game largely depended on the Army of the Republic of Vietnam, known to everyone as the ARVN. But their effectiveness was spotty. Anyone with a realistic view could see that the South Vietnamese were not stopping the NVA without American support.

The Viet Cong

In the early sixties, most of the Viet Cong fighters in the South were communist Viet Minh veterans from the successful insurgency Ho Chí Minh led against the French from 1947 to 1954. In 1954, Vietnam was partitioned at the Demilitarized Zone (DMZ) into the communist-controlled North and the democratic Republic of South Vietnam.

After the armistice, many Viet Minh soldiers moved to the North while the Catholics in the North fled to the South. As he ramped up the new insurgency against South Vietnam, Ho Chí Minh sent Viet Minh veterans south again to begin the military and terror campaign against the South Vietnamese government. Police officers, schoolteachers, and others working for or supporting the South Vietnamese government were fair game to the vicious Viet Minh terror campaign. By the early 1960s, the Viet Minh came to be known as the Viet Cong, a pejorative term that stuck through the rest of the war.

The Viet Cong moved in at night when they needed to make examples of the recalcitrant citizens and those who refused to pay them taxes by kidnapping and, in some cases, killing family members.

To stifle the VC terror campaign, South Vietnam's President Diem tried to move the civilian population in the poor areas into fort-like hamlets to protect them. It was too much like a prison, so citizens refused to occupy the hamlets, forcing Diem to abandon the strategy. The hamlets were converted to forts for the local militia.

The North Vietnamese Army began to infiltrate the South in the mid-1960s. In an asymmetric engagement, the North slowly built its forces in the South, while the U.S. and South Vietnamese never conducted a significant ground offensive north of the DMZ. The Viet Cong was a separate military organization allied with the NVA. The NVA slowly took control of military operations in the South as their troop strength increased.

As the Brown Water Navy's role in the war evolved, so did the Viet Cong's strategy to neutralize the gunboats' threat to their operation. Sapper squads began hunting down boats, setting up ambushes and drawing gunboats into them. Boat crews setting up guard posts along the canal at night had to be prepared to ambush the ambushers before they unleashed their deadly rocket-propelled grenades.

For Harding, setting up guard posts and ambushes in a powerful gunboat along the Grand Canal seemed like an adventure for a lost soul whose direction and prospects in the States were grim. But the prospect of a sudden ambush by a VC squad required a strategy to anesthetize the fear that arrived every night at sunset. It could be dicey, as his first firefight in the Plain of Reeds revealed.

To gain control of the fear that descended over his crew at night, Harding decided to accept death if it came knocking. If a blast of shrapnel interrupted his body's electrical circuits, the lights would go out, and life would be over. He engaged in this thought process any time the prospect of combat emerged. Soon, no conscious thought was needed. When ambushes on gunboats were frequent, he realized there was a good chance he was going to die. Death might be a relief from the terror of war, so he rolled with it.

Not everyone took this approach. Some never sought a strategy and remained trigger-happy, nervous nellies. Others prayed to God for passage and convinced themselves they were going to heaven if called. Harding never figured out how they reconciled their less-than-Christian behavior on liberty, but that was their problem. He did not want to be preoccupied with a daily review of his actions in a war zone to determine if he met the qualifications for entry into heaven. So, he took the fatalistic approach.

Sailors participating in Operation Barrier Reef and Giant Slingshot were playing chess for their lives on the landscape of the Mekong Delta. It was a big game, except losing was often fatal.

Most Brown Water Navy sailors served with honor despite the challenges. But a few refused to go on patrol after a close call. Some at retirement age resigned. Others washed out when their personal issues convened with the stress of combat.

STABs on Patrol

In late February, STABRON 20 boats began patrolling a stretch of the Grand Canal around Phuoc Xuyen, a little village halfway down the canal's intersection with the waterways into Saigon. The boat had no cover. Sleep was next to impossible during the sweltering heat of the day. At night, STAB crews and PBRs set up ambushes or guard posts along the Grand Canal. Two crew members caught a few winks on the gun boxes while two kept watch. Rain poured some nights, interrupting any chance of sleep as the crews huddled under their ponchos.

After three nights and four days on patrol, exhausted boat crews returned to the Benewah to stand down for a day or two. Their forward base at Phuoc Xuyen was still under construction.

STAB crews learned the ropes on patrol, inspecting sampans during the day and setting up guard posts at night to watch for NVA troop infiltrations across the Plain of Reeds. Harding began his second week patrolling STAB on Petty Officer Border's STAB. There were numerous interdictions up and down the canal and a few ambushes, so everyone was on edge.

Around 10:00 PM one night, Seaman Mike Johnson was surveying the Plain of Reeds to the north with the Starlight scope. It was a dry year, which opened more infiltration routes across the wide, flat plain. Johnson took the scope down and told Boat Captain Borders that he saw a line of soldiers in the distance. Borders asked Harding to confirm the citing.

Through the yellow-green glow of the 10-power Starlight scope, Harding saw an evenly spaced squad of about 12 people moving parallel to the canal. He estimated they were about a mile away and out of range of the gunboat. Borders radioed the Command Center, call sign Winepress, to request air support. Little did the STAB crew know, this was an NVA sapper squad and weapons porters moving into the plain to set up ambushes on Navy gunboats. They disappeared in the mist and crossed the canal undetected.

After patrolling, STAB crews returned to the Benewah to stand down for two days. They slept, ate, worked on their boats, cleaned weapons, and refueled before heading back out on patrol. Their berthing compartment on the Benewah was anything but restful. A diesel generator roared away in the neighboring compartment. Every time Harding tried to close the hatch, an engineman showed up to open it so the generator could breathe. "Keep this damn hatch open," he finally roared. Westy repeated his orders in his nasal parrot voice, "Keep the hatch open, keep the hatch open, fuck sleeping, ark."

The roaring generator was so loud it was hard to carry on a conversation, so most crew members spent their free time topside or in the mess reading the Stars and Stripes or old Newsweek magazines, which made it to this remote outpost on the Mekong a week or two after publication.

After two weeks on patrol with Petty Officer Borders, Harding was summoned by the STAB's Executive Officer, Lt. Smith. The Lieutenant told Harding to have a seat. "You are taking over the 210-boat as boat captain, beginning immediately. Petty Officer Martin has been shipped out. Your first patrol starts in two days. You'll have Martin's crew. Get them together and check out the boat. There have been some issues with maintenance."

Harding was stunned to be given command of his own gunboat as a junior petty officer with only two weeks on patrol in a STAB. He knew the routines and technology since Borders had asked him to perform all his duties as a backup. But he barely outranked the crew.

It occurred to him to ask, "Can I have Hollins as my engineman?"

"No, Hollins is being transferred to a PBR squadron to help train Vietnamese on diesel maintenance," Smith replied. "But don't tell him; I will see him later."

Losing Westy was disappointing. He had heard that the "Vietnamization" of the war was starting in the delta, and the Navy was transferring PBR squadrons to Vietnamese sailors, but he had no idea it would come to the PBR Squadron patrolling with STABs.

The SPY

Pham Xuan An[6] carefully placed the film in small canisters designed to look like little pieces of pork. Then he wrapped them in spring rolls. He had spent two hours late that night after his family had gone to bed photographing a U.S. intelligence report on the North Vietnamese Army's presence along the Cambodian border. The report documented the weapons transfers into the South and described how the NVA used their Cambodian bases as staging areas and arms depots in their strategy to build a cordon around Saigon.

Despite being a Viet Cong spy, Pham was a trusted ally and participant in the founding of the Republic of South Vietnam. He was so trusted by the South's intelligence services that he had an ID card that gave him access to the Joint Military Assistance Command (MACV Saigon), where he could obtain battle and intelligence reports to photograph. South Vietnam's Central Intelligence Office and the Diem regime relied on him for advice about the Americans' behavior and his analysis of their secret war plans written in English. So, Pham's review of those documents was not suspicious.

His covert intel made its way to Viet Cong and NVA generals. He was also the source of interdiction of special operations operating out of MACV, Saigon. He was not the only high-level spy in the South, but one of the few whose cover was never blown.

North Vietnamese intelligence was aware of the tensions rising in the Cambodian government over the communist annexation of its southeastern provinces. Officially, Cambodia was neutral in the war, but Prince Norodom Sihanouk was battling a communist insurgency in Cambodia, which he did not want North Vietnam, China, and Russia supporting, so he turned a blind eye to the North's

---

[6] The stories here about Pham Xuan An and his activities are fictional but draw from the biography about this life The Perfect Spy, by Larry Berman, Harper Collins, 2008.

occupation of the eastern provinces. Sihanouk's rivals in Cambodia were not pleased.

Pham wrote a summary of the MACV intelligence report in disappearing ink on the wrapping paper he used for the spring rolls, numbering each page so their order would be easily found. Tomorrow, he would meet an old woman, his courier Nguyen Thi Ba, at the exotic bird market on the outskirts of Saigon and offer her something to eat. She would take the spring rolls to an agent near the Viet Cong tunnels at Cu Chí, where the film canisters were retrieved and developed in a dark room. The wrapping paper was brushed with an iodine solution to reveal An's report. A courier sent the report to the NVA's base in Cambodia.

The Cu Chí tunnels were a marvel dug by the Viet Minh during the war with the French. With pedal-driven generators to provide lighting and power for ventilation, the passages ran to the Cambodian border. To avoid detection, Pham never traveled to Cu Chí. Even the old woman Ba, who was less likely to arouse the suspicion of South Vietnamese Intelligence agents, never got closer than her courier, who took the reports into the tunnels.

By 1969, Pham Xuan An, buoyed by his English skills, had risen to the top among Vietnamese journalists in Saigon. He was a respected correspondent for Time Magazine. But he had been a spy for the communist insurgents since 1947, when the Viet Minh resistance in Can Tho recruited him to the communist cause. He went undercover and ingratiated himself with the emerging South Vietnamese government during its formation in the 1950s, cultivating sources who served him well throughout his career as a spy. His cover was deep and well-guarded. He transferred battle plans and top-secret documents from MACV. The documents were so valuable that General Giap, head of the North Vietnamese Army, said, "We are now in their war room."

In the early 1950s, Ho Chí Minh predicted that the U.S. would replace the French once they were defeated. After the humiliating French defeat at Dien Bien Phú, France began its withdrawal in July 1954, dividing Vietnam in half at the 17th Parallel. The communists, led by Ho Chí Minh, governed the north. Bo Dai, the last emperor of Vietnam, who spent most of his life in France, appointed Ngô Dinh Diem as prime minister of the South.

More than one million Catholics fled from the North to the South. They were the primary constituency for Ngô Dinh Diem and his Catholic family as they began assembling a government. Most of the Viet Minh insurgents moved to the North after the armistice. 3,000 Viet Minh insurgents remained in the South to disrupt the new Diem regime. But Diem countered. From 1954 to 1956, Diem executed as many Viet Minh as he could rout out, neutralizing most of their resistance to his government.

Edward Lansdale, the famed CIA agent who led the defeat of the communist Huk guerillas in the Philippines, arrived in Saigon in 1954. His job was to develop the paramilitary forces and provide security for the South's anti-communist leadership. He helped Diem assassinate the remaining Viet Minh, consolidate power, and defeat several gangs and rival sects that threatened his government.

Even then, the U.S. State Department questioned Diem's ability to rule the country, but he had Lansdale's support, since there were few other options. The French were still trying to exercise their influence in Vietnam. Lansdale had to help Diem defeat them and recruit powerful allies. Pham and Lansdale's paths crossed when he went to work for South Vietnamese Intelligence and accidentally sent Lansdale a list of South Vietnamese agents, ingratiating himself with the CIA operative.

Pham's English skills and intellect distinguished him during this transition period in South Vietnam. He had moved to Saigon to care for his tubercular father in the early 1950s. The United States provided the French with over a billion dollars in military hardware and joined the French in their efforts to defeat the communists through the binational Training Relations and Instruction Mission (TRIM).[7] Of the 68 American officers assigned to TRIM, none could speak Vietnamese.

Pham's language skills and family connections to the Diem regime enabled him to get a job with TRIM, where he assisted with logistics and translation. Later, he joined the ARVN forces in the delta and assisted Vietnamese officers assigned to training billets in the U.S. as a staff member for the Combined Armed Training Organization,[8] all the while developing relationships that served him well as a spy. He even served as an advisor to South Vietnam's intelligence agency, the CIO.

Pham's journalism education in the U.S. also provided him with cover. In 1957, his Viet Minh spy boss approved his plan to attend Orange Coast College in California to study journalism, which the Asia Foundation would fund. An's path

[7] Ibid, page 65.
[8] Ibid, page 69-70.

to Orange Coast College was paved by none other than the CIA's own Edward Lansdale, who recommended Pham to the Chief of Education at the State Department's Mission in Saigon. Lansdale was also a good friend of the Orange Coast College President. No one suspected Pham was building his deep cover as a spy for the communist insurgency.

After completing his studies in September 1959, Pham returned to South Vietnam with dread. His direct supervisor, Moui Huong, who founded the communist intelligence network in the south, had been swept up by Diem's intelligence service, along with many other spies. He had no way of knowing if Huong had given his name away during the inevitable torture that followed his arrest. Pham had scrupulously avoided contact with other agents and communists throughout his early years as a spy in the event one of them was arrested. He had been inactive as a spy for two years while out of the country, which probably saved him. Still, he expected to be arrested upon his return to Tôn Son Nut in Saigon, so he arranged for all his family to be present when he got off the plane.

To his relief, the South Vietnamese security agents were not waiting for him. After lying low for a few weeks, Pham sought a job by contacting Dr. Tran Kim Tuyen, an old contact and powerful strategist in the Diem regime, who gave him a job in President Diem's office. Tuyen also referred Pham to the Vietnam Press, the regime's official news agency. While Pham worked at the Press, Tuyen used him to help provide cover and training for his agents going abroad who needed coaching. From there, Pham moved to a job at Reuters before finally landing at Time Magazine[9].

He served throughout the war as the most important communist intelligence asset.

---

[9] The passages about Pham Xuan An and his activities draw from the biography about this life The Perfect Spy, by Larry Berman, Harper Collins, 2008.

NVA Headquarters Cambodia

General Tran Nguyen spread Pham's report on the table in his stuffy tunnel office under the dim light powered by a bicycle light generator. Pham's analysis had been transcribed from the film at a COSVN outpost in the Parrot's Beak and transferred by courier to the NVA's Cambodian command post. It predicted an attempt to overthrow Prince Sihanouk, followed by an incursion of U.S. and ARVN ground forces into Cambodia. The timing was uncertain.

COSVN, the integrated NVA and VC party network, had revised its battle plan in early 1969. The NVA and the Viet Cong would focus on guerilla attacks using small squads. As the TET Offensive proved, the communists could not defeat the U.S.-backed coalition in large-scale battles against superior firepower with air support.

By 1970, 325,000 communist combatants and support personnel were embedded in South Vietnam. Only 26% of them were NVA.[10] They would worm their way into the society of the South and await the U.S. withdrawal.

In the meantime, the sophisticated COSVN supply effort used thousands of porters to move weapons and supplies across the Cambodian border. MACV in Saigon estimated that the NVA imported one-third of the food and 25 percent of the equipment and other supplies needed for operations in the Mekong Delta. One region in the South used over 12,000 porters. In addition to supplies, wounded communist soldiers had to be transported to field hospitals hidden in the Cambodian jungle. By March 1970, total troop strength in the provinces around the Grand Canal equaled 60,000 VC and NVA soldiers, porters, and support personnel. Thousands more occupied bases in the Parrot's Beak and Fishhook areas.

---

[10] MACV Command History, 1970, III-91 – 93.

General Tran was aware of the growing resentment among some Cambodian military leaders toward North Vietnam's presence in southern Cambodia. But he dismissed the threats to Prince Sihanouk's reign by Prince Sisowath Sirik Matak and Cambodian Defense Minister Lon Nol, an ethnic Cambodian Khmer with an animus for Vietnamese. An incursion by the U.S. and Vietnamese forces did not appear imminent if Sihanouk was in power, so Tran had no plans to modify his operations. He simply had too many weapons, explosives, and food stored in massive underground caches and not enough porters and troops to get them into South Vietnam before an invasion. He would have to defend his bases the best he could if they came after them.

Tran's outlook changed when General Văn Tien Dung in Hanoi ordered him to expedite the movement of troops and weapons into staging areas in the delta. Pham's report impressed NVA commanders in Hanoi. He was ordered to be prepared to move most of his troops to the north and west to avoid contact with U.S. and ARVN forces and their air support. The NVA would hold back defensive forces to defend the large caches located across the border northwest of Saigon. What he did not know was when and where the U.S. would attack.

Tran had to take out gunboat crews to facilitate his infiltration routes out of Cambodia into the Delta region. New Navy gunboats were setting up ambushes and guard posts along the Grand Canal. COSVN's sapper squads had been focused on Operation Giant Slingshot on the Vam Co Tay and Vam Co Dong Rivers because the National Liberation Front, the Viet Cong's government operation, was headquartered in Cambodia's Parrots Beak.

VC sapper squads, with support from the NVA, had succeeded in killing and wounding many Brown Water Navy sailors, but that had not stopped them. Instead, they doubled down on their patrols, causing Tran to temporarily move his infiltration routes from the Parrot's Beak further south to the Plain of Reeds, which was more lightly defended. The Plain of Reeds and surrounding forests were a key route into the Mekong Delta for troops and for the arms that arrived at the Sihanoukville port.

ARVN forces and the U.S. Navy's Operation Barrier Reef were disrupting Tran's operation across the Grand Canal and the Plain of Reeds. NVA troops often crossed open terrain at night when detection by surveillance aircraft was limited. During the day, when surveillance aircraft were overhead, NVA troops hid under their nets and hats, festooned with green fabric strips that rustled like rice leaves in the breeze.

The NVA's best infiltration routes were east of Phuoc Xuyen, where the tree line and jungle hugged the Grand Canal. Thatched hootches lined the canal, providing cover and protection from H&I fire. Trails, fish traps, and bunkers along the canal's banks made it a good location for swift troop movement, especially for heavier weapons like machine guns and recoilless rifles. Tran needed to open gaps in the Navy's picket line of gunboats for his final push before the Cambodian invasion.

He had learned about the Brown Water Navy the hard way. In 1969, the Viet Cong's 528 Heavy Weapons Company suffered an embarrassing loss as it attempted to cross the Grand Canal in the Plain of Reeds, where it was interdicted by PBRs. After the NVA company's retreat, it was decimated by Navy Seawolf gunships, losing a prized 12-tube, 107 mm rocket launcher[11]. A similar loss occurred on Christmas Eve 1969 when Tran hoped the Americans were celebrating the holiday. 200 NVA troops were forced to retreat when they were caught by gunboats crossing the Grand Canal. This embarrassment was the final straw for Tran. He needed to assign his own sapper squad on the Grand Canal to take out more gunboats.

Communist sapper squads were specially trained saboteurs and special forces armed with a variety of weapons and explosives for surprise attacks on the U.S. and South Vietnamese. Tran's sapper squad arrived along the banks of the Grand Canal in early 1970. This squad worked with VC agents, whose network of scouts identified the location of boats using signals from oil lamps.

General Tran learned of the STABs' arrival while planning the push to transfer troops and weapons stored in tunnels along the Cambodian border. The STABs' low freeboard made them harder to see at night. STAB gunboats had only been on the Grand Canal for a few days when they interdicted NVA troops attempting to cross the canal near An Long.

NVA scouts had been unable to see the lone, low-profile STAB nestled against the 3-foot-high bank. STAB 217 caught the lead NVA scout and gunner trying to cross in a sampan under the cover of darkness and opened fire. Petty Officer Brewster called in air support. Sea Wolves swept in with mini-guns and Zuni's, causing the NVA to disperse and head back into the side canals and fish traps

---

[11] Edward J. Marolda and R. Blake Dunnavent, Combat at Close Quarters, Warfare on Rivers and Canals of Vietnam, Naval History and Heritage Command, U.S. Navy, 2015, page 52.

with their wounded, Chinese machine guns, AK-47s, and ammunition cans. Other PBRs and STABs rallied to join the fight and guard the flanks of the primary engagement.

A few days after the interdiction, two of General Giap's attachés visited General Tran at his base. They were shuttled in from Phnom Penh disguised as rice merchants. They were there to discuss rumbling from their intelligence services about an invasion of their Cambodian sanctuaries by MACV's forces. They berated General Tran for being defeated again by U.S. Navy gunboats, even though their interdiction had only cost two dozen lives and stalled the infiltration by a few days. It was symbolic of their impatience. Furthermore, the construction of an Advanced Tactical Support Base at Phuoc Xuyen seemed to indicate that the U.S. was not backing down from their interdiction of troop movements into the delta.

Giap's attachés discussed strategy in light of the potential coup and an invasion by U.S. and ARVN forces. They ordered Tran to advance his infiltration of troops into the Delta region across the Plain of Reeds and the areas east of Phuoc Xuyen, which were lightly defended. Other NVA units would attack Cambodian forces to the north and west to take Phnom Penh before the invasion. Tran would hold back some forces to defend the massive weapons caches and bases.

In the scheme of things, Tran had much more to worry about than a handful of Navy gunboats on the Grand Canal, but he desperately wanted to embarrass Admiral Zumwalt, who commanded the U.S. Brown Water Navy. The STAB squadron was Zumwalt's pet project. He hoped that the casualties would lead to abandonment of the ATSB at Phouc Xuyen. Tran knew he could no longer rely on unpredictable Viet Cong squads. Zumwalt and the STABs would pay for his latest embarrassment.

Tran ordered his sapper squad into the Phuoc Xuyen area in early March to plan a crippling attack on the Grand Canal's gunboat picket line. He had visions of the STAB's gasoline tanks exploding in a great fireball that would cause another U.S. retreat and might take them off the river altogether. The images of this fireball enthralled Tran's sapper squad. They were outfitted with a recoilless rifle, rocket-propelled grenades, flares, and camouflage. Captain Minh was assigned to lead them. Minh set up a base of operations from a secure village just over the border with escape routes back into a Cambodian sanctuary if a Seal Team or Special Ops squad came after them.

By early March, Minh's squad was in place with canal access to the Plain of Reeds and the woods east of Phuoc Xuen. They warmed up with an ambush of a "heavy" in the wood line east of Phuoc Xuyen. With the help of the local Viet Cong cadre, the squad moved into a hootch along the canal. From the hootch, scouts pinpointed the position of Navy gunboats as they moved into position at dusk. On this night, a modified landing craft armed with 20 mm cannons and 50-caliber machine guns presented a fat target.

The night was dark as pitch. Half of Minh's squad moved down a fish trap to within 50 feet of "the heavy" while three squad members with rocket-propelled grenades set up in a hootch on the upstream side. Precisely at 8:35 PM, RPGs ripped into the gunboat from the hootch but did little damage as the rounds were broken up by rebar and detonated in the foam lining the sides of the craft. As the heavy guns rotated to port, saboteurs ran from the fish trap on the starboard side and threw a satchel charge onto its deck. The explosions damaged the landing pad, killed a Vietnamese Navy liaison, and wounded two sailors. Tran's squad slipped away in the fish trap as 20 mm rounds zinged wildly around them.

This attack was just a warm-up. A week later, Minh's squad took out a PBR, killing two sailors and seriously wounding another. Then, his squad left the Phuoc Xuyen area to the safety of their border camp to regroup, rearm and plan for their attack on a STAB. Minh was ordered to meet General Tran at a remote base across the border.

The Cambodian Coup, March 1970

General Nol and Prince Sisowath Sirik Matak had secretly discussed a coup to oust Sihanouk for months. Prince Matak was Cambodian royalty and a rival to Prince Sihanouk. Nol was a proud Khmer with a deep hatred for the Vietnamese, who had attacked and occupied Cambodia throughout its history. Legends of Vietnamese atrocities and humiliations of Khmers were Cambodian folklore embedded in the culture and handed down from generation to generation. So, it did not take much effort to inspire Khmers and their young followers to protest against the North Vietnamese.

Nol was not quite all in. He wanted the Vietnamese out of Cambodia but had reservations about deposing Prince Sihanouk and his royal family, which still enjoyed significant support, especially among rural peasants. Nol hoped to generate enough public pressure to convince Sihanouk to abandon his neutrality without being deposed. But Nol also knew the Cambodian military would need U.S. assistance and weapons to fight the Khmer Rouge and the North Vietnamese Army, which Cambodia could not defeat alone. Sihanouk's thinly veiled duplicity would not deliver those weapons from America.

In early March, after Sihanouk's departure to France, loudspeakers on the lamp posts around Phnom Penh began broadcasting speeches deriding the presence of the North Vietnamese in southeastern border provinces. Matak and Nol convinced Nol's brother to organize large protests in Phnom Penh, led by students, government workers, and contractors. On March 8th, Nol closed the port of Sihanoukville to the North Vietnamese and gave the communists 72 hours to leave the country. On March 11th, the North Vietnamese embassy was attacked by a crowd of protesters. Vietnamese businesses were sacked.

Nol's reluctance to oust Sihanouk evaporated when Prince Matak recorded a press conference in Paris where Sihanouk threatened to execute both Matak and Nol upon his return. Prince Matak set the wheels in motion in the General Assembly for Sihanouk's ouster. On March 17th, troops were stationed at street corners throughout Phnom Penh. On March 18th, Sihanouk was officially ousted as President and Prime Minister by the Cambodian General Assembly.

Now, Nol had no choice. He assumed emergency powers and began making plans to seek retribution from the Cambodian Vietnamese, whom he thought were allies of the North Vietnamese. He gave the green light to the American and South Vietnamese invasion into the eastern provinces to rout out NVA sanctuaries.

Meanwhile, the backlash against Nol's coup spread among rural Cambodians who viewed Prince Sihanouk with the reverence of a deity. Sihanouk had nurtured a cult-like following among rural villages along the Mekong. During the rainy season, he gave speeches in villages promising to reverse the river's flow to demonstrate his powers. When the snowmelt and monsoon rains flooded low-lying areas, the high tide in the South China Sea forced water back up the Mekong River all the way into Cambodia. The Mekong's reversal could be predicted with tide charts, which Sihanouk used to stage events at his appearances in rural villages. Sihanouk proclaimed in his speech that he could reverse the Mekong's flow. His procession then threw bright yellow flower pedals into the river as the flow reversed. He promised the crowd he would also use these powers to convince the spirits to deliver a bountiful harvest to their village.

Villagers knew the Mekong backed up without Sihanouk's influence, but the pomp and circumstance, along with a few influencers planted in the crowd, persuaded poorly educated villagers to believe in the Prince's powers. Struggling farmers desperately needed hope to cling to, and Sihanouk gave it to them. If the harvest failed, Sihanouk used Russian and Chinese money to deliver bags of rice to hungry villages.

As word of Sihanouk's ouster spread, rural peasants erupted in violent protests, killing Nol's brother, whom they caught while he was traveling through the countryside. The army reacted by shooting protesters. Ten years of Cambodian genocide had begun.

Captured

After Harding took over as boat captain of the 21 boat, Westy was assigned to a PBR squadron. The entire PBR squadron was scheduled to be transferred to the Vietnamese Navy at the end of the month as part of President Nixon's Vietnamization of the war. To everyone's dismay, the PBR boat captain, 1st Class Petty Officer Eastman, fell off the dock on the Benewah into the swirling waters of the Mekong and never resurfaced.

Westy, who had experience with PBRs from his training in February, was appointed temporary boat captain and assigned to a relatively cushy patrol in the Mekong River around the Benewah and the YRBM barracks ships anchored between An Long at the mouth of the Grand Canal and the Cambodian border. Harding's crew recovered Eastman's swollen body three days after he drowned. It was just 200 yards from the Benewah, held there by the reversal of the river's flow during high tide.

During Westy's first week, his PBR rafted up with a PBR from YRBM-16. They floated down the Mekong, inspecting occasional water taxis and sampans. During one of these raft-ups, he learned about the Last Chance Saloon, a shack on a barge tied to YRBM-16 near the Cambodian border. PBR sailors invited him to join them for a poker party on Wednesday night at the Saloon.

During off-duty hours, boat captains had the authority to take their boats out for testing, which the crews also interpreted as "for recreational purposes." On March 5th, Westy took his PBR up to YRBM-16, about 2 miles from the Cambodian border, to join PBR sailors playing cards and drinking at the Last Chance Saloon.

Westy arrived around 3:30 in the afternoon and met a fellow Kentuckian who escorted him to their card table. The game's rules were to drink a shot of Jim Beam if you won a hand. By 5:00, Westy had won two hands, drank shots, and downed two beers.

Realizing he had to make it back downriver to the Benewah before sunset, he stopped playing cards and retired to a corner of the shack to nod off for a few minutes.

"Hey dude, wake up!" shouted Petty Officer Jenkins. "It's 6:00 o'clock. You need to head downriver. Are you okay?"

"Yeah, yeah," Westy replied. "Help me get underway."

Jenkins escorted Westy to the dock and untied the PBR while he started the engine and engaged the pumps. He was still a little tipsy, but he could make it downriver, he thought.

He idled out into the river. Something wasn't right. The river was much wider than when he arrived. He turned around to head back downriver, reversing the direction from his arrival. After clearing the YRBM, he motored up and put the patrol boat hull on plane. He thought he heard a voice shouting as he sped away but ignored it.

While Westy was asleep, the Commander of YRBM-16 had repositioned the barracks ship using a motorized pusher barge, reversing its position in the Mekong. Occasional repositioning of the barracks ship was required to prevent the enemy from calculating coordinates for mortar attacks and mines. The bow of YRBM-16 now faced downstream. Unaware of the reversal, Westy headed upstream into Cambodia.

At 25 knots, he crossed the Vietnam-Cambodian border within a few minutes. As the river narrowed, a panic swelled inside him. He was lost. He nosed the PBR into the bank with the pumps engaged and stood on the starboard gunnel to take a leak before he reversed course.

Suddenly, automatic weapons fire ripped into the PBR hull. Westy dove into the river and surfaced with his hands up as rounds zipped into the water around him.

Shadowy figures stood above him on the bank with their AK-47s pointed at him. Their leader, the tallest of the group, raised his hands to stop their fire. In the distance, another diesel-powered boat was approaching. Two of the guerrillas slid down the bank and motioned with their weapons for Westy to scramble up to the trail, where the leader hit him in the stomach with the butt of an AK-47. He bent over in pain and puked while he was grabbed by the collar of his fatigues and pulled into the brush along the river. They pushed him along the trail with their rifles for about 100 yards to escape the approaching Cambodian patrol boat. Then, his captors took his watch and tied his hands together at the wrist with twine.

Westy thought the Viet Cong had captured him. Little did he know, he was a prisoner of the ruthless Khmer Rouge, the Cambodian communist guerillas allied with the North Vietnamese Army. For half an hour, he was pushed along a trail through the forest onto a road, then back into the forest to a clearing. A faint glow in the west was all the daylight that remained when he arrived at the edge of a camp. They led him along the edge of a camp downhill for 50 yards to a small clearing. In the dim light of their torches, he saw three t-shaped crosses in a line. Limp bodies hung from two crosses. Their feet were off the ground, and smoke rose from the ashes of a small fire under them. His captors tied his arms to the horizontal timber of the unoccupied cross and took his boots.

"At least my feet are on the ground," he thought. He was relieved when his captors left without any further violence, but he knew a rough night lay ahead.

The mosquitoes began attacking as darkness settled in. With his arms bound, Westy tried blowing them away from his face, wiggling his head, and flexing his jaw. Nothing seemed to work. Finally, torrents of rain washed them away. He took the opportunity offered by the storm to pee in his pants, which were soaked and would be rinsed clean in a few minutes. He was cold. His bound arms had been hurting, but now they were numb. Mercifully, he passed out.

He passed in and out of consciousness throughout the night. At one point, he awakened to the stench of rotting flesh riding in the breeze. So, he breathed through his mouth and nodded off again for a few minutes. He stood on his toes to relieve the pressure on his arms for as long as possible and wiggled his hands to stimulate blood flow. When he wasn't fighting off the pain, he randomly thought of how he could escape. He had to get back to the river.

To escape his physical discomfort, he thought about his life back home, his dad playing bluegrass on his Martin guitar. He reviewed the events that led him to this predicament, which surely seemed to be the end of his life.

Inevitably, his thoughts strayed to the day his brother ran around the back of the school bus and was hit by a drunk driver who ran through the bus stop sign. He heard the whack as Thomas' head hid the hood of the 1955 Mercury. He ran down the road to find Thomas's unconscious body in the ditch, with brain fluid oozing from a hole in the side of his head. Westy knew he was dying.

Thomas fetched the mail every day when they came home from school to take it to his mother, who was busy with a toddler and a newborn baby, in addition to the two growing boys. It was Thomas's expression of love to his mom to fetch the mail for her, which was often overdue bills his dad struggled to pay. His mom offered a loving smile, nonetheless.

Westy ran into the house to find his mom putting candles on his sister's birthday cake. "Mom, Thomas has been hit by a car!" he shouted.

"Westford, don't joke about something like that," his mother replied.

"I am not joking!" Westy saw the panic on his mother's face as she ran out the front door. "Call the Smiths," she said.

Westy wept from these recollections and the stress of the day's events. He could never forget his mother's look of desperation holding Thomas' crumpled body in the back seat of the Smith's car. Mr. Smith had wisely decided to meet the ambulance. But it was too late. Thomas died on the operating table shortly after arriving at the hospital.

After Thomas died, Westy lost the ability to concentrate on his schoolwork. He flunked out of the 5th grade and struggled through the 6th and 7th grades. He found salvation in rebuilding lawn mower engines. Although he could barely read above the 5th-grade level, he advanced to rebuilding car engines in shop class by the 9th grade. At the age of 17, still a year behind, his hot rod was the envy of every redneck in Pike County. When it crashed in a street drag race, and he was arrested, the judge gave him the option of six months in jail or joining the military.

Desperate for recruits, the Navy accepted Westy in a unique program for the poorly educated and slow learners. To the Navy's surprise, he excelled in the test of his mechanical abilities and was sent to engineman's school.

Finally, Westy's thoughts turned to escape strategies, and considering his background, he realized that playing dumb to his captors might be his way to get them to drop their guard.

Morning dawned on what he thought might be the last day of his life. He was awakened by the voices of the Khmer Rouge gang coming down the hill. They arrived with two litters and long machetes drawn from their scabbards, which he surmised were going to be used to hack him to pieces. Instead, two Khmers went to the back of the crosses where the two bodies hung. They cut the twine binding the bodies to the crosses, which fell to the ground in a hump. Westy saw their charred feet and ankles, which had been roasted by the fires to ensure they could never escape afoot. The man's entrails were hanging out of a large gash in his lower abdomen. The bodies were carried off in the litters through a little clearing, which he realized must be the grave site and the source of the rotting flesh smell.

Westy had resigned himself to his execution by these thugs, so it was surprising when they used the machetes to cut the twine that bound him to the cross. He fell to the ground, unable to move his arms for a moment. The Khmers lifted him to his feet, bound his hands in front of him, and walked him back up the hill to a clearing in the forest canopy. There, four black-clad soldiers and six porters were waiting for his arrival. Six bundles of AK-47s lay at the porters' feet. One of the officers spoke to the Khmer leader, who nodded.

After giving Westy a couple of swigs of water from a canteen, the soldiers led him away. It took a few minutes on the trail for Westy to process this transaction. It dawned on him that his captors had traded him for several bundles of AK-47s. But he still did not know who they were.

After an hour, the entourage arrived at a clearing under the forest canopy. Westy was thrown into a cage-like cell by his new captors. Another soldier brought him a change of clothes, which were black pajamas like those worn by the Viet Cong. Still, they smelled better than his soiled fatigues. A bucket in the cage was filled with water, but it had scum floating on the surface. He scooped it out, hoping that rain would replenish it. Another pail was in the other corner. It smelled like urine, so he surmised that was his potty.

Westy sighed in relief at these new confines, which were far from elegant but were much less threatening than the previous night's scene, with two bodies hanging from crosses. He knew he was still in Cambodia and had concluded correctly that he was now a captive of the North Vietnamese Army.

The Interrogation

Westy spent three days in the cage before anyone contacted him, which he thought was strange. He was fed one bowl of rice with a few flecks of fish with fish sauce, given to him through a small door the guard lowered. He held his bowl up and held it through the door to request fresh water so he did not have to drink the putrid water from the bucket. But they grunted at him gruffly and shook their heads, "không," which Westy knew meant "no."

An NVA officer visited the cage in the afternoon of the third day and introduced himself as Captain Minh. In Vietnamese, he ordered the guard to open the gate and bind Westy's hands with bands. Both guards accompanying the officer had bayonets affixed to their AK-47s. In remarkably good English, the officer introduced himself as Captain Minh and told Westy to follow him but keep his distance, or the guards would kill him with their bayonets.

The group hiked along the trail through the triple forest canopy. Westy counted about 600 barefoot steps before they entered an area cleared of underbrush under a large canvas canopy adorned with the little green strips of fabric that made the area look like grass from above. Half a dozen ominous-looking soldiers stood at the corners. One of the guards unwrapped the bands around his wrists. A table with four hand-built stools sat at the back of the cleared area. It looked like a mobile headquarters with nothing that could not be moved quickly.

A high-ranking officer sat behind the table. Captain Minh walked behind the table and sat on another stool. He told Westy to sit on the stool at the front of the table.

"Hello, seaman Hollins, meet General Tran," Minh said. General Tran had traveled down Highway One from his headquarters further north to meet this captured American. Westy was a rare catch for the NVA's Cambodian operation.

"Seaman Hollins, we have a few questions for you. Your cooperation will result in favorable treatment," Captain Minh said. "Why do you take PBR into Cambodia?"

"I reckon I got lost," Westy said, accentuating this Appalachian accent as part of his play-dumb strategy. Westy was an engineman, not a seaman, but decided not to correct them.

"What do you mean by this reckon?" Captain Minh asked. Westy realized these NVA officers may not understand his dialect or Appalachian expressions. He would double down on their use to confuse and appear illiterate.

"Reckon is what I thought," Westy replied.

Then Minh said, "We know that you on STAB boat." Westy was shocked. "You engineman. Where gas tanks in STAB?"

General Tran and Captain Minh wanted as much information about the STAB configuration as possible to ensure the success of their upcoming sapper squad attack. He suspected the gas tanks were under the floorboards but was testing Westy's cooperation.

Westy tried to lie, "In the back, by the engines." Minh interpreted his remarks to General Tran.

"That lie, Seaman Hollins," Minh yelled. "You cooperate, or we put snake in your cage at night!"

"You and STAB crews kill civilians in Phuoc Xuyen. You sign confession, and we release you," Minh said, thrusting a paper at Westy in one hand with a pencil in the other. Westy looked at the confession. He knew it was bad, and survival training had prepared him for this ruse.

Westy marked the signature line with an "X" and returned it to Minh.

"What this X?" Minh yelled.

"I cain't read or rye-it," Westy replied, accentuating his accent. Captain Minh looked puzzled momentarily and began talking in Vietnamese to General Tran.

Westy did not know that during the days since his capture, General Tran had exchanged encrypted radio messages with Viet Cong agents in Cu Chí, who sent a courier to advise the old woman Ba of Hollins's capture. Ba met Pham An at the market and asked him to get information on Hollins. There was talk at

MACV and a communique about Hollins' capture, so his position with the STAB squadron was easy to discover. MACV was also considering a special op to rescue him. An relayed the message to Ba, who met a VC agent with the information and provided the background from the MACV communique, which was radioed to Tran.

"You sign a confession, or we put the snake in your cage," Minh threatened again in a loud voice.

Hollins signed with another "X." "I told you I cain't read or rye-it!"

"We send you to Hanoi Hilton!" Minh yelled, waving for the soldiers to return Westy to the cage.

While sitting up with his back against the wire wall that night, Westy heard the hinges of the little door squeak. The shadow of a guard was stuffing something through the door, which he heard plop on the cage floor. It was the snake Minh had promised — a six-foot python.

During his youth in eastern Kentucky, Westy and his friend captured rattlesnakes for sport. A preacher in one of the fundamentalist churches learned of Westy's penchant for rattlesnakes and asked him for one for his snake-handling sermon. He believed he could pray to God and be protected from the snakebite, which he would demonstrate to the congregation while requesting contributions that would confirm the church's righteousness and help prevent harm to their pastor. During the service, the preacher was surprised when he was bitten and had to be rushed to the hospital. He survived, which he would later tell the congregation was by divine intervention, but he never used the snake sermon again.

Westy knew to sit still to prevent that snake from being aggressive. The snake might seek his warmth, but if he did not move, the risk of a bite was not great. He did not know if this snake was venomous, but he could not take any chances. When the snake slithered around his ankle and wrapped around his leg, he knew it was probably just a python and not poisonous or big enough to be a threat, just a scare. Westy grabbed the snake just behind its head and killed it by slinging its head into the side of the cage. The following morning, he held it up for the dismayed guard with a big smile.

That day, another interrogation resulted in the same outcome. This time, Minh threatened to put rats in Westy's cage if he did not cooperate. That night, he heard the little door open again and four more plops, which he suspected were the rats. He spent the night shooing them away as he thought about how to handle the rats.

While on patrol one day on the Grand Canal, Westy saw a woman selling rats from a cage in her sampan near An Long. The cage hung over each side of the narrow sampan, with two dozen rats scurrying around inside. She was moving slowly along the canal as residents came out of their hootches and waved her to the bank to order fresh rat for dinner. She complied with their orders by reaching into the cage, grabbing one by its long tail, and breaking its neck with a quick snap.

Westy waited until morning. He was weary from lack of sleep. The rats were more disturbing than the snake.

At first light, with the guard watching, Westy baited the rats with a few grains of rice, caught each one by the tail, and broke their necks with a snap, mimicking the action of the rat merchant on the Grand Canal. The guard smiled and opened the little wire door, pointing to the dead rats. He wanted them to supplement his diet. Westy complied, stuffing dead rats through the door into the guard's hands.

Then he held up his water bowl, which the guard graciously refilled from his canteen. He had made a friend, which would pay dividends later.

Westy had become a curiosity at the camp. Soldiers traipsed by to glimpse him like a new animal at the zoo. On the fifth day, Westy noticed two women and a man with a guitar bag walking by the compound. One of the women looked at Westy in the cage, making eye contact with him. Surprisingly, it was like she was trying to make a connection. She was stunningly beautiful, even in her drab uniform.

After a couple of hours, the party returned up the trail, and she made eye contact again. This time, Westy smiled widely, exposing the gap in his two front teeth. Before she dropped her eyes and looked away, he saw a flash of a smile in return. If there was ever love at first sight for Westy, this was it.

The Singer

Hanh Phú sat in camp, sharpening her machete with a whetstone. She had arrived at Tran's Cambodian camp after a trek down extensions of the Ho Chí Minh Trail. Her plan was nearly complete, and she had collected a few items necessary to execute it.

Hanh Phú was a singer in an NVA musical troupe. She was the NVA's equivalent of a USO performer. Her primary mission was to improve morale. Hanh Phú sang patriotic songs that inspired soldiers from the North to endure the hardships of the war to achieve final victory over the colonial oppressors from the West. Her beauty and sweet voice were enough to mesmerize soldiers longing for female companionship.

Since arriving at an NVA waystation, she had been secluded in a special encampment away from other troops, protected by bodyguards. Except the Major in charge of her troupe was anything but protective. During the trek south through Cambodia, an airstrike forced them to flee from the trail. She thought Major Lê was pulling her to safety. Instead, he pulled her into the high grass and forced himself on her until she had no choice but to submit to his sexual advances.

Now, six weeks later, she was pregnant and feared for her life. Word had come down that her troupe would move into South Vietnam sometime in late March or April before the expected invasion by U.S. and ARVN troops. She did not want her baby growing up in a war zone, and she did not want to live in a camp under threat from Major Lê. She would defect if given the chance, but only to the Americans. The South Vietnamese could not be trusted.

When the American prisoner showed up in camp, her anger and her plans to defect grew each night as she lay in her hammock. She began to think of using the American to escape. She knew she did not have much time before the American was shuttled north to a POW camp, so she began casually surveilling the area where he stood in the cage, making eye contact unobtrusively while passing by.

The American prisoner seemed to have a relationship with one guard, unlike the others. The guard would give him water from his canteen instead of making him drink from the bug-infested bucket. This was the guard Westy had given the rats to.

Finally, the day came to execute her plan. It was risky, but she did not care since surviving the infiltration and the war in the South was uncertain. She waited until sunset when the guards changed, and the one most friendly to the American took over.

Hanh Phú hid in the bushes near the cage. When the guard was not looking her way, she raised her head for the American to see and then ducked behind the bushes. Westy recognized her as the one who had made the curious eye contact.

"What was she up to?" he asked himself. The next time she raised her head, she held a machete next to it and gestured with her hand across her throat, then ducked behind the bush again. The guard noticed Westy focusing on something and looked around but saw nothing.

"Could she be planning to kill the guard?" Westy wondered incredulously.

To brighten his spirits, Westy had begun singing songs occasionally, but not so loud that the guard would be irritated. Now, he started singing "Oh Susannah" loudly to get the guard's attention and held up his water bowl, hoping to get a refill from the friendly guard's canteen. The guard walked over, prepared to oblige, but pointed to Westy's mouth and said, "không," which meant for Wesley to shut up.

As the guard moved to open the little door to the cage, Hanh Phú sprung from around the bush. Westy sang louder to mask the sound of her movement. She ran ten yards with the machete raised. The guard heard her at the last minute and turned just in time to have his forehead and nose split open by the sharpened machete. He fell back against the cage. Westy grabbed the back of his uniform through the wire door to prevent him from attacking, as Hanh Phú delivered a slashing blow to his left knee, causing him to collapse. He dropped his hands, allowing her to deliver a deadly blow to his neck, severing his trachea and carotid artery. Blood spurt from the womb as his body lay twitching. She hit him in the skull one more time for good measure.

Hanh Phú sheathed her machete, grabbed the guard's keys and unlocked the cage. She picked up his AK-47 and ammo belt, giving it to Westy to carry. They had seconds now to escape before someone entered the area. They dragged the guard into the cage, closed the gate, and then ran into the darkening woods, where she stopped after a few yards. She reached into the rucksack and handed Westy some oddly shaped sandals, which he put on his feet with her help. Then, she led him through the woods with her machete drawn, but only to cut vines when necessary so as not to leave a trail.

After 100 yards, they reached what appeared to be a clearing. It was a series of bomb craters from a bombing run. Hanh Phú led Westy through the woods, paralleling the series of craters. He wondered why she didn't make better use of the cleared-out area. When he stepped into the edge of the woods into the dirt, she pulled him back and shook her head, which Westy understood meant not to walk in the dirt.

Then, after a few yards through the woods, she moved over into cratered earth and waved for Westy to follow as they doubled back in the direction they had just traveled, except this time, they were making tracks in the disturbed ground. Westy was puzzled but followed as she cut between two bomb craters and entered the woods on the other side of the craters, where she stopped for a second to point down at their tracks. They were oddly going away from them in the opposite direction of their travel. Westy turned the sole of one sandal up to see the toe box where the heel should be. The tread was reversed. "How clever," he thought. It made their tracks look like they were going in the opposite direction from where they were walking.

Hanh Phú said, "VC shoe." She had acquired the sandals from the Viet Cong, who guided her party down the trails through Cambodia.

As they re-entered the woods, they could hear voices approaching from the wooded area on the other side of the bomb craters. Hanh Phú signaled for Westy to follow and moved deeper into the woods to hide behind bushes to avoid detection. Hanh Phú tapped Westy on the shoulder, and as he looked into her eyes, she smudged mud onto his white face for camouflage. All he could think was how beautiful her eyes were.

The voices came closer. Four NVA soldiers were walking along the line of craters in the dim light, obviously looking for the escaped American. They stopped when they saw the tracks, fooled by the reversed sandal prints, and hurried off in the wrong direction.

Hanh Phú quickly got up and signaled for Westy to follow as she moved stealthily through the woods, occasionally looking at the sky when there were gaps in the canopy, as if she was receiving direction from the stars. Night was falling, and there was no moon. Westy wondered how they could make it through the dense forest in the dark when a clearing came into view. She turned to follow the tree line along the rice paddies, staying under the canopy as much as possible. They must have walked for an hour. When the dark outline of a village could be seen. She signaled for Westy to follow as they skirted around the village and re-entered the woods. Westy sensed the Mekong was just ahead, but it was too dark to see.

Hanh Phú obviously knew where they were. She had visited the village as an emissary for NVA commissary buyers, who bartered for fish at the market. She signaled for Westy to lie down and put her finger over her lips to signal silence. She gestured for the AK-47, then left, turning for a moment to see if Westy was trying to follow.

Westy lay still to see if she would return. A flare went up over the village shortly after Hanh Phú's departure, which told Westy that hostile forces were ahead. Hanh Phú returned after half an hour. She pointed to the village and shook her head, indicating the presence of hostile forces.

She gestured for Westy to lie down again and rest while she sat on watch with the AK-47 at the ready. There was nothing he could do now. His fate was in her hands. His mind wandered. If they reached safety and returned to the States, could he marry this woman? That seemed like paradise at this point. He fell asleep.

He was startled awake when he heard a branch crack. It was Hanh Phú returning from another scouting foray. Too many tortured nights in the cage had worn him thin. She signaled for him to get up and led him along the tree line, staying clear of the village. Westy expected to hear dogs barking, then realized that they had probably all been eaten. It was still dark, but a very faint glow signaled the sun would be rising soon. They skirted around the village and down the bank to the Mekong. She waded into the water and gave Westy the AK-47. She began floating downstream, bumping her feet on the bottom to stay afloat. Westy followed her. After about 50 yards, a dozen sampans appeared tied up to the bank.

Hanh Phú stood up in the waist-deep water and held the sampan while Westy untied the bowline. She moved forward and Westy helped her into the boat. He swung the stern around to the bank and got in. But it was so tipsy it flipped, and he dumped her out. One more attempt and they were on board safely,

He picked up one thin paddle and used it to begin maneuvering the sampan into the current. This sampan had no motor, which was fine, since motor noise would only attract attention. As the sampan caught the current, Westy looked back to see a shadowy figure up on the bank, but he was unarmed, thankfully. It was still too dark to see if he was uniformed. He hoped they could make it across the border before sunrise.

Hanh Phú slung the AK-47 across her chest and picked up a pole to help navigate. Westy's paddling skills required steering assistance, so she used the poll to keep the sampan off the riverbank as they moved downstream. Westy did not want to get out into the dangerous currents of deep water but was having trouble maneuvering through the eddies along the bank.

In the dim light, he did not see the Cambodian Navy patrol boat until it was too late. It was tucked into the bank behind a tree down in the river so it could not be seen from upstream. The sampan was almost broadside the patrol boat when one of the sailors shouted and pointed at Hanh Phú with the AK-47 strapped around her. He opened fire with a 50-caliber machine gun, blasting her out of the sampan and cutting the thin craft in two. Westy dove into the water and swam toward Hanh Phú. He could hear rounds zinging into the water, and then the shooting stopped. He touched her body and pulled it up to him. A round had gone through her chest and torn through her heart.

Westy clutched the limp body and started yelling, "You killed her, you assholes! You killed her! You killed her!" He was sobbing. He no longer cared if he got shot. The Cambodian boat captain ordered a cease-fire when he heard the English, realizing Westy was an American. The mud had washed from his face.

Westy released Hanh Phú's body and watched it drift away downstream. The patrol boat idled up to him and offered him a boathook, which he pushed away. A blast into the water with an M-16 brought him to his senses. Even though he did not recognize the Cambodian flag, he knew the NVA and Khmer Rouge did not have patrol boats on the Mekong. The captain killed the engine, and two crew members pulled him over the transom.

The boat captain spoke a little English. "You American soldier?" he asked.

"I am U.S. Navy," Westy replied. "You killed her!" he yelled and lunged toward the boat captain. Two sailors wrestled him to the deck, and a third one handcuffed him.

"She NVA!" the boat captain exclaimed loudly.

The engine started, and the boat idled out into the current before starting upstream at full speed. Westy was going to a Cambodian jail in Phnom Penh.

On Patrol, Grand Canal, South Vietnam

Shortly after advancing to boat captain, Josh Harding was promoted to 2nd Class Petty Officer. His boat crew consisted of two third-class petty officers and a seaman. Daniel Rizzinato was the 3rd Class Petty Officer and gunner's mate in charge of the boat's weapons. Engineman 3rd Class George Wilson took care of the engines, and Seaman Boatswain's Mate Rusty Carter was the jack of all trades, who kept the boat fueled and stocked with ammunition, water, and C-rations while helping Rizzinato with the guns. No one could pronounce Rizzinato's name, so everyone called him "Rizz."

Rizz had been transferred into the squadron from Operation Giant Slingshot. He had seen a lot of combat in his six months on patrol along the Vam Co Tay River. More experienced than the STAB crew, he was very condescending, often acting as if he was their superior. Harding knew trouble was brewing with his assignment to their boat.

The STAB crews had heard that Westy was missing. A Cambodian patrol boat had found his PBR with a line of bullet holes across the bow. They relayed the information to MACV in Saigon, where it was assumed he had been killed or captured.

Meanwhile, the forward base at Phuoc Xuyen was still under construction. Into March, the relentless patrolling without any place to sleep was taking its toll on the crews. Twelve STABS and a few PBRs were assigned positions at night to watch for NVA infiltrating from Cambodia. Boats were stationed about a kilometer apart along the canal east and west of Phuoc Xuyen.

During the day, the sun was merciless, making sleep impossible unless it was cloudy and not raining. During rain squalls, crews huddled under ponchos since the STAB boats had no cover, just a small open cockpit with no room for anyone to lie down except to curl up on one of the two-gun boxes on the starboard and port side of the boat well.

Early in their deployment, STABs interdicted a troop movement trying to cross the canal at night just west of Phuoc Xuyen. The STAB was concealed against the bank in a little cove and virtually invisible in the darkness to the NVA reconnaissance scouts sent forward of the platoon. The platoon walked right up on the boat, which opened fire at 20 yards. The next day, the crew swept the area and found an abandoned pack with a diary, women's clothes, and a guitar. Blood stains on the pack confirmed that the bearer had been wounded or killed. South Vietnamese Navy liaisons discerned from the diary that the STAB crew had shot up an NVA entertainment troupe. It was the troupe from which Hanh Phú had deserted.

Harding took his responsibility as boat captain seriously, so he refused to sleep at night until he could no longer resist the urge to catnap for a few minutes. He stayed awake most of the night while one crew member stood watch with him and two others slept for two-hour stints on the gun boxes. Rizzinato created dissent when he insisted on sleeping past his two-hour sleep segment, occupying one of the gun boxes for an extra hour. At 3:00 AM, Harding and Rizzinato almost came to blows when Harding woke him up and forced him to stand watch.

After two weeks of this routine, Harding had to do something. His crew was worn out. They had not interdicted any enemy troops, but the relentless patrolling without sleep was pushing crews to the breaking point. He had decided to complain to the Executive Officer about the conditions at the end of the last patrol when they returned to the Benewah to stand down for two days.

But when he got to the dock alongside the barracks ship, Lt. JG Danny Schmidt met him. "I have been waiting on you, Harding. I need you and Franklin's boat to join me on a special mission into Cambodia. It's an extraction, but I can't tell you any more about it. You are not to divulge any information about this mission to other crews. It will take the rest of the day to complete. Get your boat fueled."

Harding's plan to complain about fatigue and the patrol environment evaporated completely as "special op" adrenaline kicked in to shut down his fatigue. He loved special ops. He ordered the crew to refuel the boat and hurried to the quartermaster to get C-rations for the crew.

Within 30 minutes, STAB 210 was headed up the Mekong at 40 knots, destination Neak Leung, Cambodia. This mission was what STABs were designed for—a stealthy operation that would never be recorded in the history books. Even Harding was unaware he was participating in a mission to free Westy from capturing and delivering a Cambodian Navy Commander to a secret meeting on YRBM 16 to plan the Cambodian invasion.

Bonjour

Agent Homer Gentry's Pilatus landed on a crude airstrip outside of Neak Leung, where he met Bill Watson, a junior CIA officer. Both were carrying concealed pistols. Gentry had a briefcase full of twenty-dollar bills totaling $5,000. Watson had been negotiating with Colonel Kou and Commander Charya Vinh of the Khmer National Navy for Westy's release. The negotiations had started before Sihanouk's official ouster but found new urgency once he was deposed.

Such negotiations customarily required paying bribes to open doors, a norm known to Cambodians as "bonjour." A position in the Cambodian government was a tacit license for graft. Businesses understood and expected it, so they built it into their pricing. Bonjour made negotiations easier for the CIA, since overcoming objections usually only required sweetening the pot. Colonel Kou had given the green light to Commander Vinh to finalize the negotiations for Westy's release to Gentry.

But Vinh had his demands, one of which was relayed to Gentry by CIA agent Watson. Gentry had to provide the jailer $1,000 in U.S. dollars, which was no problem. But Commander Vinh wanted $4,000 for his role and to pay off others to ensure a smooth transfer. Someone in the chain of command also needed a tractor. Gentry would gladly pay it as part of the deal, but he also wanted Vinh's cooperation in the upcoming Cambodian invasion by U.S. forces, which was still top secret.

Before the STAB's arrival, Gentry and Watson met Vinh to finalize the plan for Westy's release and to discuss ferrying Vinh downriver on a fast STAB to YRBM-16 for a meeting with Admiral Zumwalt's Deputy Chief of Staff. The meeting was designed to show respect for Vinh and plan for the U.S. Navy's operations on the Mekong during the Cambodian invasion. Use of the sleek STAB would demonstrate their capabilities and help Vinh understand the role they could play in securing the Mekong for the Cambodian Navy.

Running at full speed, the two STABs reached Neak Leung in just over an hour. Harding had heard automatic weapons fire on two occasions during the transit, but the gunfire did not seem directed toward them. Upon arrival, Lt. Schmidt disembarked from Petty Officer Franklin's STAB and met Gentry and an interpreter on the banks of the Mekong. Vinh did not speak English, so one of the CIA's Cambodian agents accompanied Gentry throughout the operation.

Vinh stood beside them on the riverbank with a radio. He held the small duffle filled with 20-dollar bills that Gentry had given him earlier. Vinh, Gentry, the interpreter, and Schmidt walked him over to Harding's boat, which Vinh boarded with a big smile.

Both STABs departed and were on plane headed south on the Mekong within seconds. Vinh laughed throughout the trip downriver. The STAB was twice as fast as any river patrol boat in his Navy. After arriving at YRBM-16, Vinh got off the STAB and onto the dock, where he met Lt. Finnegan, who escorted him to the captain's quarters.

During the dinner meeting, Vinh wanted to talk about the boat ride and whether Cambodia could acquire a few STABs for his Navy. Admiral Zumwalt's aide, Captain Moses, said it was impossible since only 20 boats had been manufactured. As the dinner progressed and he consumed more French wine, Vinh agreed to allow the U.S. Navy to operate patrol boats up the Mekong during the Cambodian invasion. They would assist Cambodia in reclaiming control of the waterway from the NVA and block the NVA's escape routes once the invasion by ARVN and U.S. Army forces commenced.

Back in Neak Leung, Westy had been delighted to see Gentry arrive at the airstrip after Vinh's departure. Gentry had the aura of a man in charge of the operation. Maybe he would remove the handcuffs. But there was no greeting, and the handcuffs were not removed before they boarded the Air America plane to Tôn Son Nhut. Westy realized Gentry's stoic demeanor spelled trouble, which was confirmed when Westy was positioned between two ominous-looking agents who were openly carrying pistols. The Military Police were waiting for him in Tôn Son Knut, where Westy was arrested and charged with dereliction of duty and misuse of government property. He would spend the next few months in the brig at Nha Be, preparing for his Court Martial.

NVA Headquarters, Cambodia Late March 1970

General Tran unrolled the intelligence report from Pham An. With Sihanouk out of the picture and Lon Nol firmly in control, the U.S. had finalized its negotiations to invade the NVA's Cambodian sanctuaries. The report said that U.S. and ARVN ground forces were planning an invasion in late April or early May.

With their ally Sihanouk out of the picture, the NVA had begun disruptive operations against the Nol's forces in Cambodia to protect their flank and as a safeguard against a pincer operation that would find their forces trapped between the Cambodian army attacking from the northwest and the MACV forces coming up from the south and east.

Following orders from Hanoi, in a move the north would later regret, the NVA, Tran, for the first time, began transferring substantial tranches of weapons to the Khmer Rouge to fight Nol's Army. Ironically, the North's alliance with the Khmer Rouge was strengthened by the coup and advanced the destabilization of Cambodia.

General Tran did not need An's report to speed up the transfer of weapons and troops into the South. When the protests began in Phnom Penh against North Vietnam's occupation of eastern Cambodian provinces, Tran ramped up transfers across the border, but a lack of porters and troops limited what he could do. Given the sheer size of the weapons and material caches, there was simply no way to get it across the border and nowhere for it to go. After a surprise invasion by ARVN forces in February deep into the Parrot's Beak, Tran shifted his troop movements to the southwest across the Grand Canal, where the Navy's newest gunboats awaited in ambush.

ATSB, Phuoc Xuyen

On March 18th, the day the Cambodian parliament officially ousted Sihanouk, Brown Water Navy PBRs and STABs interdicted two NVA companies trying to cross the Grand Canal near An Long. In the ensuing firefight, one STAB sailor was mortally wounded while conducting reconnaissance on the bank. He died three weeks later in a hospital in Cam Ranh Bay.

Harding was not on the canal during this engagement, which occurred in daylight hours, which was a sign of Tran's desperation to move troops and weapons before the invasion. As word of the battle spread around the Benewah, Harding went topside to see large plumes of smoke from airstrikes rising up east of An Long.

Later that afternoon, the quartermaster advised boat captains to be prepared to spend three nights up the canal while on patrol. Construction of the Advance Tactical Support Base (ASTB) was nearing completion. The ASTB at Phouc Xuyen would serve as berthing and refueling while on patrol.

By base standards, like the ASTB at Son Ong Doc, the Phuoc Xuyen base was tiny and vulnerable, consisting of a few barges embedded in the bank of the Grand Canal with tin-roofed shacks serving as berthing quarters, a mess hall, a fueling depot, a watchtower, and docks for STABs and PBRs surrounded by a perimeter of concertina wire. Most of the base area was flooded in the high-water months of spring. So, a wooden catwalk was built to provide access to the watchtower, where a mortar emplacement was set up to defend the base and fire H&I rounds into the nearby wooded area.

Harding and his crew left the Benewah for Phuoc Xuyen the day after the An Long firefight. The relentless patrolling had worn down his crew, and he looked forward to seeing the new, advanced base. Having a place to sleep during the four-day patrols up the Grand Canal would be a great relief.

Shortly after arriving at Phuoc Xuyen, Harding met the cheerful construction chief Seabee Chief Petty Officer Andrew Brady, who wanted a ride in the fast

STAB boat in exchange for a tour around the ATSB. Brady told Harding about the challenges of building the base in the swampy, lowland mud. He said he had two more days in Phuoc Xuyen before returning to the States, where he looked forward to seeing his new grandson, who was born during his year of deployment.

He walked Harding around the wooden catwalks and up to the watchtower in the middle of the base. They climbed to the top, where a sixty-millimeter mortar and M-60 were set up. Two sailors stood watch 24 hours a day atop the tower, looking out across the vast Plain of Reeds for enemy troops. Harding thought it was a weak defense for a base that could be overrun at any time if the VC decided to attack. There were no perimeter guards, but open fields around the base made them susceptible to air attack.

At least once per hour at irregular intervals, the sentries on the watch tower dropped a round in the mortar tube and sent it into the tree line about 250 yards from the perimeter. This was typical harassment and interdiction fire, a practice designed to deter the enemy from assembling for an attack. Sometimes, it seemed that more H&I rounds were fired in Vietnam than in combat.

As STABs and PBRs began using the Phuoc Xuyen base, a gaggle of Vietnamese women in sampans showed up in late afternoon to sell sodas and ice as the boats prepared to embark on their night patrol. Boat crews used ice blocks in boat coolers to keep water and other libations cool. A cheerful, young orphan girl who spoke remarkably good English was among the peddlers. She sold orange sodas and colas she had somehow acquired, which, along with her outgoing personality, made her a favorite of boat crews.

As operations at the base ramped up, some psychological operations genius decided that a few STAB sailors should visit the village of Phuoc Xuyen on a goodwill visit. The villagers were Hòa Hảo, a sect of Buddhism, and unquestionably anti-communist. Adherents had opposed the French occupation as well and, later, the Viet Minh's attacks on civilians. The Hòa Hảo sect was founded in 1939 by charismatic Huỳnh Phú Sổ, whom adherents considered a saint. His revered position among a sizable portion of the population threatened the communist's plans for dominance of the South's society and elimination of their religious practices, which rivaled allegiance to the communist state. In 1947, Huỳnh Phú Sổ was kidnapped by the Viet Minh and killed, fixing Hòa Hảo opposition to the communist insurgency in the South. Despite their opposition to the Viet Cong, The Hòa Hảo at Phuoc Xuyen were still subject to VC intimidation.

Harding and his engineman were chosen to join two others from the 214 boat to meet the village chief and walk around the small hamlet meeting residents. Harding agreed to participate but felt uneasy after he was told he could not carry a weapon.

After meeting the elder, he and three others began walking around the hamlet with Lt. Schmidt. They were not to make contact but just walk around smiling as if they were friends. What was the point, Harding wondered? Kids usually ran up to Americans begging for chocolate from their C-rations. But for some strange reason, all the villagers retreated to their hootches as four sailors in fatigues began walking around the hamlet. The locals who were out avoided eye contact. Lt. JG Schmidt realized something was amiss and quickly led Harding and his group back to the ATSB. Of all the junior-grade lieutenants Harding met during this enlistment, he ranked Schmidt as the smartest.

The next week, the Viet Cong entered the village at night and kidnapped the orphan girl, who sold orange sodas, as punishment for the village's brief courtship with American boat crews. She was never seen again. The message to the villagers was that they would pay a price for cozying up to the Americans. The village chief ordered STAB's Commander Perkins to avoid contact with the villagers, so crews were forbidden from entering the village afterward. The women still showed up in the afternoon to sell their ice and sodas, but their time was limited to half an hour each afternoon.

The young girl's kidnapping was the VC "welcome wagon" to the gunboat crews at the new Phuoc Xuyen base. But it was not the only disheartening event. The day before he was scheduled to depart Phuoc Xuyen and fly back to the States for his return to civilian life, Petty Officer Brady was killed instantly when an H&I mortar round from the watch tower fell short and exploded on the surface of the canal next to the barge where he was standing.

On Patrol Grand Canal

As primitive as it was, the forward base at Phuoc Xuyen was a vast improvement for gunboat crews. After coming off patrol around 7:00 AM, boat crews ate breakfast and hit the sack until around 2:00 PM, when lunch was served. Five or six hours of sleep in a day was a welcome improvement.

After lunch, crews begin preparing their boats for the night patrol. Hardy was stunned to see beer sold by the base quartermaster at a "happy hour" for a nickel a can just three hours before they departed on patrol. He decided not to drink for fear that a firefight would erupt while on patrol, and he wanted to have all his wits about him. A few older guys were overindulging. Harding was worried about the consequences, which were revealed on the second week of operations out of the Phuoc Xuyen ATSB.

At 5:30 PM, boat captains assembled at the base's command center, call sign Winepress, for their assigned coordinates, which was the general location to set up their guard post on the canal for that night. During the briefing, intel about the enemy's movements was shared, and they were given an encryption module to scramble their boat's radio communications so the NVA and VC could not intercept them. The Officer of the Day had warned that intelligence revealed the presence of a VC sapper squad operating in the Phuoc Xuyen area to take out gunboats.

It was General Tran's squad. Their mission was to open gaps in the gunboat picket line along the Grand Canal so he could move his troops and weapons across the canal into the South before the Cambodian invasion.

Gunboats pulled into the bank of the Grand Canal at sunset and set up "guard posts," also known as a "water-borne ambush." A phalanx of Navy gunboats along the Grand Canal created a picket line: one gunboat stationed about a kilometer apart for 20 kilometers.

As Harding learned from his training with PBRs, in some locations along the canal's south bank, the crews had to set up a machine gun nest on the other side of an elevated road about 50 yards away from the boat. The road prevented the crews on the canal from seeing the enemy coming out of the high grass.

Before the STABs arrived, a Viet Cong squad had taken out a PBR in an ambush that moved into position behind the elevated road. From then on, boat crews set up a machine gun nest just over the road, out of sight of the boat, to interdict ambushes. Two sailors on what was facetiously called "the beach" were alone in the dark all night with a Starlight scope, a machine gun, an M-79 grenade launcher, and a portable radio to communicate with the gunboat back on the canal bank.

On this night, Harding was assigned coordinates about ten kilometers from the advance base at Phuoc Xuyen. It was his third patrol as a boat captain, and the enemy was about to test his leadership skills for the first time.

He pulled the boat into position where a few hootches occupied the elevated road on the south bank. A gap in the hootch line gave him fire lines without worrying about too much collateral damage to civilians if a firefight erupted. He sent Rizzinato and Wilson to set up a machine gun position over the road with the portable radio, Starlight scope, and M-60 at sunset. Harding and Carter stayed on the boat to watch the north bank.

Harding had received little training for most of this action. It was "on-the-job training." They often inspected vessels and looked for contraband. But there was no way to restrain the VC if they encountered them. There were no handcuffs. If they resisted, all one could do was shoot them.

Unknown to Harding, a VC agent using an oil lamp in a hootch on the road signaled their boat's position to Tran's sapper squad waiting a few hundred yards away. The squad was prepositioned south of the canal, waiting for a signal that a gunboat had moved into position. This would be a reconnaissance mission for the squad, which had been ordered to move a few clicks the next day to set up ambushes in the tree line east of Phuoc Xuyen. Tonight, their goal was to observe the STAB crew stealthily before darkness fell to watch for any weaknesses that would improve their chances of a successful, catastrophic attack. If they had a clear shot, they would take it, but that was not the plan.

The NVA had determined from its own intelligence that U.S. commanders in Washington were showing weakness in the face of casualties and massive student protests. The loss of a STAB gunboat might curtail the Navy's eagerness to sacrifice any more sailors and withdraw from their disruptive patrols.

The PBR squadron had been turned over to the Vietnamese Navy, so their presence was no longer a reliable threat. Their presence had been reduced to irregular daytime patrols. One PBR had already sunk when the Vietnamese crew clipped the bank at full speed. Other PBRs were inoperable because the Vietnamese Navy was not following maintenance protocols. Now, Tran just needed to knock out the STABs and get as many weapons transferred across the Plain of Reeds before the expected invasion.

As the sun set in the west, Harding was monitoring the incessant chatter on the radio from Petty Officer Barton, who was on his second tour as a boat captain. He had overindulged at beer call. As punishment, he was not allowed to take his boat outside the base perimeter that night, which insulted and infuriated him. Barton's radio chatter to Winepress was interrupted when the portable radio broke silence with a request from Rizz to open fire on an enemy squad approaching their position. He wanted immediate authorization to open fire.

The Harding got a radio call from Rizz that an enemy squad was approaching their position. He wanted immediate authorization to open fire.

Protocol required Harding to get permission to open fire from the Officer of the Day at Phuoc Xuyen, but he could not break through Barton's stronger signal.

Harding keyed his radio mike again, "Winepress, this is Racing Danger. Request permission to open fire; we have a squad approaching our position, over!"

No response, so Harding radioed again. "Winepress, squad advancing on position, request permission to open fire," he pled. All that came back was more whining from Barton to Winepress about how he was on his second gunboat tour and was not doing any good hanging out inside the base perimeter.

Harding ordered Carter to go over the road to get Rizzinato and Wilson.

Seconds after Carter left the boat, all hell broke loose with outgoing tracer fire from Rizzinato and Wilson. It looked like they were shooting high. The firefight stopped briefly when Wilson and Rizzinato hightailed it over the road, clamoring back aboard the boat, visibly shaking. They had abandoned their weapons in retreat. The unflappable Carter was a few steps behind them, carrying their radio, which he had wisely thought to retrieve.

As Carter approached the boat, he went down as an RPG round exploded behind him. Harding thought for sure he had been hit, but he had stumbled at the same time the round exploded, which saved his life. He barely missed a step as he jumped aboard the boat with the radio in hand.

Rizzinato and Wilson were still shaking but had not been wounded miraculously. Harding was very worried about losing the Starlight scope. He called Winepress for air support as he moved the boat away from the attack to a new position away from the hootches. He was going to send someone out to get the Starlight scope and M-60, but Winepress told him there was too much risk with an airstrike on the way.

A Seawolf helicopter gunship made contact a few minutes later. Harding directed him where to lay down fire. It was too late to do any good, but the mini-gun and Zuni rockets put on a nice show of fireworks. Harding wondered how the villagers felt about the war's sound and fury at their backdoor. The kids probably loved the fireworks.

Harding and his crew returned to the ambush site early the following day. The abandoned weapons and the Starlight scope were right where they had been left. Amazingly, neither the enemy squad nor the villagers had taken them. Losing the Starlight scope would have given the VC or NVA much-needed night vision.

Two nights later, Harding was assigned a position east of Phuoc Xuyen in the tree line interspersed with hootches. As he moved into position, Engineman Wilson, who was still jumpy from the ambush the night before, claimed he saw a uniformed officer on the canal bank in a gap in the tree line. Harding had become skeptical of Wilson, whose nervousness on patrol had reached a new level after the firefight.

Harding asked Carter to grab an M-16, and the two of them jumped onto the canal bank, crouching on either side of a trail that led away from the canal.

A big bunker had been dug into the bank a few feet in front of the boat. It was an obvious infiltration route. The bunker was used to scan the canal for gunboats before the NVA crossed it. Maybe this time, Wilson wasn't mistaken. But Harding did not see anyone, so they returned to the boat. Harding moved the boat away from the bunker and set up about 40 yards away, where he could watch it all night. Just as they moved into position, two sampans came down the canal. Harding summoned the young men in the sampans over to the stern of the STAB. It was just too coincidental.

Harding knocked his M-16 into the water as he moved into position to examine their IDs. In perfect English, one of the young men offered to retrieve it for Harding. "No!" Harding replied emphatically. He suspected they were VC, scouting the boats' position along the canal, but they produced IDs and were unarmed, so there was nothing he could do but let them go. After they left, Harding stripped and submerged himself in the four feet of water to find his M-16. The night passed uneventfully.

A few days later, a STAB crew caught an NVA platoon crossing the canal at this location. A firefight erupted, and the NVA retreated, fearing an airstrike. The next morning, the STAB crew recovered a Chinese machine gun left behind in the hasty retreat. Usually, abandoned gear meant that the wounded had to be carried away instead of weapons.

On the following night, Harding's patrol included Lt. JG Schmidt, riding along as the patrol officer, who had command of the entire ten-boat patrol on this section of the canal. He directed Harding to set the boat into the bank in a heavily forested area with banana palms and a few hootches scattered under the forest canopy. Harding did not like the position since it was at the mouth of a dry fish trap, a ditch dug perpendicular to the canal for 100 yards. It was the perfect infiltration route and sneak route right up to the boat. A hootch was set back off the canal on the boat's port side, further complicating the position if a firefight erupted. It would be hard to get permission to open fire in an area ripe for civilian casualties.

The night was overcast and pitch black, with no moon or stars illuminating the Starlight scope's images. The scope was useless except for scanning the windowless hootch emitting a glow between the palm fronds thatched together for walls. A baby in hootch was crying incessantly. With the Starlight scope, Harding could see the shadow of a man moving inside the hootch, obviously agitated. The crew sat quietly with their M-16s at the ready. Something was wrong.

Suddenly, Schmidt, Wilson, and Rizzinato stood erect and fired their M-16s down the fish trap in unison just as Harding heard footsteps running toward the boat. Harding threw a hand grenade into the darkness, which caromed off a tree limb and blew out the side of the hootch. Because of his hearing loss, Harding had not heard the footsteps until the NVA scout neared the boat. It was so dark the scout had not seen the boat and had almost run right up on it.

Silence followed. There was no movement or sound from the hootch. No baby crying. Harding wondered where they had gone. Even if they had run out of the hootch, he should be able to hear the baby crying.

Harding muttered aloud, "If I killed that baby, I am never coming back out here."

"Shut up," Schmidt responded. Then, he ordered Harding to move the boat about 50 yards away from the mouth of the fish trap.

"Why didn't we do that in the first place?" Harding thought to himself. It was not the first time he had wondered if a young Navy officer lacked common sense, but Schmidt was usually on top of things.

There had been no time to request permission to open fire with the imminent threat to the crew. Unknown to them, they had intercepted one of General Tran's scouts, looking for a gap in the gunboat picket line to guide his NVA company and weapons across the canal.

The night ended without further incident. Harding was glad to return to the Benewah the next day to rest for two days. On the transit down the canal back to the Mekong, they passed ARVN troops on the elevated road in the Plain of Reeds. An ARVN officer gave Harding's boat the finger as it passed by. "And these are our allies," he thought to himself.

He still wondered about the baby in the hootch. He assumed that if the family had been wounded or killed, the locals would have sought medical care or notified the village chief unless they were VC. Still, it was disconcerting.

Upon arriving at the Benewah, Harding learned of a special operation being planned by Commander Perkins to run a canal near Dong Tam that Navy gunboats had never navigated. He sent a note to the Executive Officer, volunteering his boat for the two-boat run. Although the operation was supposed to be high risk, as fate would have it, volunteering for it may have saved his life.

On the afternoon of April 2nd, Harding's boat and STAB 218, with Commander Perkins aboard, cruised down the Mekong. Twelve STABS were up the Grand

Canal patrolling that night out of Phuoc Xuyen, and six boats were standing down for two days of maintenance at the Benewah.

The Dong Tam base was sprawling compared to the ATSB at Phuoc Xuyen. It looked like a muddy mess with a perimeter and guard towers interspersed throughout the compound. After chow, the crew read magazines and chatted with other Navy personnel about their war experiences before turning in at 10:00 PM. They had been in the sack for about 15 minutes when a loud explosion sent everyone to the floor. After a few minutes, it was apparent that only one round was incoming, so everyone began stirring, wondering what the hell had happened.

A base guard entered the dim barracks and told everyone to keep the lights off and return to bed. The VC had dropped a mortar round into the barracks next to them, blowing the leg off one Marine and wounding a couple of others.

Harding wondered how the VC could precisely put one round into the barracks. He learned later that a VC agent working undercover at the base as a housekeeper was arrested by a South Vietnamese Intelligence operation. He had walked off the distance to the base gate and then took a right-angle walk to a location for the mortar. From there, the VC used simple geometry to calculate the distance from the barracks to their mortar position. The barracks were clustered, so dropping a round into the complex was a cinch.

The casualties in Dong Tam were nothing like the carnage unfolding on the Grand Canal that night.

Ambush

Minh's sapper squad, with their Viet Cong guides, moved from the south bank to the north bank of the Grand Canal in broad daylight using two sampans to conceal their rocket-propelled grenade tubes under the floorboards. The movement across the canal took less than five minutes as they entered a fish trap and disappeared into the forest. The STABS were off the canal during the day, and the ARVN were not around, so movement by a small squad was undetectable.

Captain Minh moved the squad into a location concealed by banana palms and dense brush. There, they would wait until night fell. Two Viet Cong agents disguised as fishermen were on the bank of the canal. They would watch for the STABS' arrival at sunset and pinpoint the boat that would be attacked that night.

Chief Petty Officer Farmer was the patrol officer in STAB 213 on this night. The boat moved down the canal at a low wake speed to avoid upsetting sampans along the bank. Farmer ordered the boat captain, First Class Petty Officer Harold Moore, to move 213 about halfway down the 12-kilometer area where the boats were setting up one kilometer apart. Farmer did not like setting up his guard post in this section of the canal. There were too many hootches to conceal the enemy and constrain his defensive fire.

After night fell, there was a sigh of relief since most enemy ambushes occurred at dusk before night concealed the low-profile STABs. Mosquitoes swarmed around the crew. Rain squalls and low clouds rendered the Starlight scope useless, except for looking around the hootches that were lit inside. Around 11 o'clock, the 213 crew heard a commotion on the north bank about 60 yards away in the direction of a hootch they had been watching. Through the Starlight scope, Gunner's Mate Masters could see the shadows of men moving around inside the hootch. Chief Farmer ordered the crew to put on the flak jackets and radioed Winepress to request permission to open fire. The request was denied because of the presence of "friendlies."

Farmer was exasperated. Now, the crew could hear muffled voices. Farmer ordered Masters to shoot a flare over the hootch, which risked exposing his position, but he had to consider moving the boat in light of the threat. The flare arched over the canal, flickering its eerie white light across the canal but revealing nothing. As it went down and the light faded, dead calm fell over the canal. Then, through the quiet, the sound of metal sliding together raised the hairs on the backs of the STAB crewman. They looked at one another.

Minh had commandeered the hootch and run the family out at twilight after his scouts identified their target. He knew the STAB crew would never get permission to open fire on a hootch along the canal. The first sound the 213 crew heard were the protests as the couple who lived there gathered a few belongings and trudged into the rain.

Darkness made the STAB, nested against the bank, impossible for Minh's crew to see. He would have to use a flare and instructed two squad members with B-40s to hide outside behind each corner of the hootch. Another sapper set up inside the hootch, aiming through an opening. Minh extinguished the oil lamp and readied a flare, which would signal the start of the ambush and illuminate the target for this squad.

Farmer radioed Winepress again and, in a low but emphatic voice just above a whisper, said, "Damnit, I need permission to open fire. We hear voices. Sounds like a squad is setting up across the canal."

"Negative 213. If you see anyone with weapons, let me know," Winepress responded.

It was just after midnight when Minh's flare ignited over STAB 213. The second the boat's hull was illuminated, the sapper inside the hootch fired his RPG into the side of 213. The armor-piercing round sliced through the light armor and flak curtain and exploded in the crew well, blowing Engineman Anderson's head off. Shrapnel blew through the torsos of Masters and Boatswain's Mate Echols. They were bleeding in the bottom of the crew cockpit when the second round exploded in the back of the cockpit, sealing their fate. Shrapnel also shattered Farmer's right arm. The third round hit the hull at the waterline and blew up next to the self-sealing fuel cell, which did not explode into the fireball Minh had promised his squad. Remarkably, Boat Captain Moore, sitting in the cockswain's seat just three feet away from the KIAs, was uninjured.

Chief Farmer and Petty Officer Moore's ears were ringing from the explosions, and they were in shock, but Moore was able to start one engine on the boat. "Get us out of here," Farmer yelled to Moore as he directed fire from an M-60 into the hootch. His right arm was bleeding profusely and dangling by his side. The first B-40 round had cut the controls to the starboard engine. With only one engine, the boat whipped around in a circle back into the bank. With Farmer still spraying the opposite bank with 7.62 mm rounds, Moore got control of the boat and motored at half-speed back up the canal toward Phuoc Xuyen.

Moore got on the radio: "Winepress, we have been hit. Three KIAs. One more wounded." Send Medivac. Other STABS were already underway to render assistance.

STAB 215 got to 213 first and pulled alongside the stricken boat. The 215 crew moved Farmer into their boat and applied direct pressure and a tourniquet to his hemorrhaging arm. Boatswain's Mate Goodings got into the crew well, slipping on the blood that covered the floor. He was stunned by Anderson's headless body, still oozing blood from the stump of his neck. Shrapnel had torn through the flak jackets of the others. Their gaping wounds meant they bled out quickly.

Winepress had designated a landing zone in anticipation of an attack and directed the crews to one just east of Phuoc Xuyen. Petty Officer Moore was shaking like a leaf but refused to get on the Huey flying Farmer to surgery. He wanted to stay with the bodies of his dead crewmen and accompany them back to the Benewah after the evacuation copter arrived with body bags. He was pulled away from the 213 and reluctantly boarded the chopper, flying to the APBY near An Long.

Under flashlights held by other crew members at the scene, Goodings and four other crewmen from responding boats stuffed the broken bodies into body bags. They did their best to put the flesh and body parts into the right bags, but there was no way to tell, really. The skull fragments with hair on them obviously belonged to Anderson. Goodings' blood-stained fatigues and boots would be discarded later, but the experience haunted him for the rest of his life.

Special Operation Canceled

In Dong Tam that morning, Commander Perkins came into berthing quarters to meet the crews from the two STAB crews scheduled for the special operation.

"I am canceling the special operation. We had three crew members killed last night on the canal. We can't take any more casualties at this point. Get some breakfast and meet me at the dock at ten hundred to head back upriver," Perkins said.

Harding was disappointed to hear that the special op was canceled, but he understood why. It was a somber journey up the Mekong at full speed. When the boats returned to the Benewah, the 213 boat was already out of the water, resting on a barge. The rocket motor body, with its fins intact, was wedged against the fuel cell, where the hull had been removed to examine the damage. Two holes were visible where the B-40 rounds had penetrated the side of the boat and entered the crew well. Most of the blood had been scrubbed out of the boat, but some blood remained on the ties at the bottom of the flack curtain.

The next day, Harding's boat was headed back up the Grand Canal to Phuoc Xuyen for another three nights on patrol. At the boat captain briefing, Patrol Officer Deaton said that a sweep of the canal by ARVN forces after the ambush found two blood trails and abandoned B-40 tubes, indicating that Farmer had miraculously managed to wound or kill two sappers as they scurried away.

Defensive Measures

Harding had no trepidation about returning to patrol after the fatal ambush. His boat would have been on patrol that night if he had not volunteered for the special operation. With only ten or 12 boats on the canal the night of the attack, the chance that his boat might have been the one hit was uncomfortably high.

On this first night back on patrol, he was assigned a position as far down the canal as he had ever been from Phuoc Xuyen. Unlike the bare areas around the Plain of Reeds, the forest cover here was thick but sparsely populated. As he reached the assigned coordinates, a medieval-looking mud-walled fortress loomed ahead on the south bank. He surmised that it was a base for the ARVN or local militia. It looked like an old strategic hamlet built in the early sixties when President Diem tried to move citizens into compounds to protect them from the Viet Minh's campaign to murder and terrorize citizens in the South. Harding drove his boat down to get a close look at the primitive structure before turning around to put some distance between his position and the fort.

He pulled into the north bank about 150 yards from the fort. There were no hootches in this stretch of the canal. It was a little spooky. The forest canopy was higher than in most areas around the canal but somewhat open on the forest floor. After being in position for 15 minutes, a report from a 105 mm barrel came from the direction of the ARVN compound, followed by a round whistling in on the boat's position. The crew ducked below the gunwale for protection from shrapnel. The round blew up in the forest, just out of range of the deadly shrapnel. But the incoming round was close enough that the spent shrapnel could be heard raining back down in the nearby trees. They were lucky that they were not out of the boat doing reconnaissance. Was this harassment fire from our allies? Harding radioed Winepress to report the incoming from the base and demanded the Vietnamese cut it out. It was one more signal that our so-called allies did not want us in their country.

This was the last single-boat guard post on the canal for Harding and his crew. After the ambush and three KIAs, Commander Perkins sent a request to Naval

Command that two boats be sent out to each guard post instead of one. This action would cut STABs' interdiction range in half, and the disruption of NVA forces across the Grand Canal would be limited. But Perkins knew that the Cambodian invasion was imminent, and he could not personally justify sacrificing any more lives, especially since it was apparent that the U.S. had begun to turn the war over to the Vietnamese. Most U.S. forces were expected to stand down or leave before the end of the year, anyway. What was the point of sacrificing more lives for a lost cause? And writing letters to the families of KIAs was the hardest thing he ever had to do.

The ambushes did not stop entirely, but they were never as successful again as on that April night. A new, unanticipated danger emerged with the initiation of the two-boat guard posts: the prospect of friendly fire from the boat across the canal.

Two weeks later, Harding's boat and the 214 boat were positioned together east of Phuoc Xuyen when Engineman Wilson claimed he saw someone in uniform standing on the opposite bank. Harding radioed the 214 boat but got no response. He took the Starlight scope from Wilson and confirmed the head and shoulders of someone standing in the brush on the opposite bank. There was no weapon visible, but someone was scouting the area, looking in the direction of where the 214 boat was supposed to be set up. Except that it was not visible.

Harding called in a request and got permission to open fire immediately. Winepress had stopped denying requests to open fire after the successful ambush on April 3rd. As he aimed the M-60 across the canal and clicked off the safety, Harding told the crew if anyone was going to pull the trigger, it would be him. Just before opening fire, he asked Boatswain's Mate Carter to keep an eye on the target with the Starlight scope. He would not pull the trigger until Carter saw a weapon.

Suddenly, Carter said, "Hold your fire. It's the 214 boat," which floated out of bushes at the last second. The boat's gunner's mate was standing on the engine covers on the back of the boat, hidden in the willows on the other side of the canal. Harding had been seconds away from pulling the trigger.

The patrol ended without further incident, and the 214 boat never realized how close they had come to being raked by friendly fire. The following morning, Harding and his crew cruised back down the Grand Canal to the Benewah, resting in the wide and relatively peaceful waters of the Mekong.

Cambodian Genocide

Harding was in the berthing area of the Benewah when a sailor ran in, exclaiming, "Bodies are floating down the river. Come topside to look!"

Harding rushed to the railing as 500 swollen bodies floated by, bobbing in one mass. After a few minutes, another group of 300 drifted by in the Mekong's current.

The next day, when the tide reversed the river's flow, the corpses came back upstream, broken up into smaller groups surrounding the ship like a death stew.

The bodies were young men from the areas around the village of Churi Changwar. Lon Nol's forces had rounded up ethnic Vietnamese, tied them together, and executed them with machine guns. The massacre was Lon Nol's retribution for his brother's murder, further motivated by his hatred for ethnic Vietnamese, whom he viewed as allies of the North Vietnamese invaders.

The North Vietnamese Army began to attack Cambodian government forces at the end of March. By early April, they had taken control of portions of the Mekong River south of Phnom Penh. With their ally Sihanouk deposed, the NVA were now destabilizing an unfriendly Cambodian government led by their enemy Lon Nol. Nol responded by attacking ethnic Vietnamese, many of whom had fled to Cambodia from the Mekong Delta during Ho Chí Minh's war with the French.

A decade of genocide began with the Churi Changwar massacre. After Nols' defeat by the Khmer Rouge communists in 1975, Pol Pot's nightmarish rule ushered in "The Killing Fields," which resulted in the murder and starvation of one and a half million Cambodians.

The Bamboo Road, May 1970

In 1966, with help from Cambodian agents, the CIA documented the emerging importance of the Cambodian port of Sihanoukville to the infiltration of enemy weapons into the delta. Three years later, their report determined that between December 1966 and April 1969, Chinese vessels had delivered at least 21,600 tons of military and 5,300 tons of nonmilitary cargo to Sihanoukville, from where it went by truck convoy over Cambodian roads to drop points near the Mekong. From there, trucks and porters moved the weapons to the North's underground depots on the border.

The military stores distributed through the Sihanoukville port included 222,000 individual and 16,000 crew-served weapons, a haul sufficient to equip 600 enemy battalions. The operation would ultimately transfer over 100 million rounds of ammunition and over half a million mines and hand grenades to the NVA and Viet Cong dumps hidden underground in the Mekong Delta Region.[12] Enough weapons could be shipped through the port to supply the entire NVA and Viet Cong military operations in III and IV Corps in South Vietnam. The Hak Ly trucking firm moved the weapons by road from the port to the Cambodian towns Svay Rien and Kampong Rau in Kien Phong province, where porters and the Viet Cong took them to underground border caches.[13]

MACV had long asserted that Sihanoukville was a primary route for logistical support of the VC/NVA forces into the Mekong Delta Region of South Vietnam. The Ho Chí Minh Trail was primarily used to supply the forces in three corps regions of the country.[14] The trail had been steadily improved since 1959 when the 559th Transportation Group started its work improving it. Eventually, the 559th would employ 50,000 troops and 100,000 laborers to build truck roads and bridges across streams through Laos into Cambodia. Sophisticated anti-aircraft

---

[12] *MACV: The Years of Withdrawal, 1968–1973, pg 303.*

[13] *The Cambodian Incursion, Brigadier General Tran Dinh Tho, ARVN, Maclean, VA, 1978, page 21.*

[14] *MACV: The Years of Withdrawal, 1968–1973, pg 304.*

systems were stationed along the route to fend off the relentless bombing by the U.S. The 559[15] had most of the bombing damage to the trail repaired within a few days of the attack[15].

To halt supplies into the Delta region, U.S. forces had to break these supply lines and, close the port at Sihanoukville to communist ships and strangle the communist strategy to encircle Saigon if they had any hope of winning the war. Nixon's secret bombing campaign had not stopped the flow of weapons, so an invasion into the NVA's Cambodian sanctuaries was the last resort.

Over the past three years, MACV's plans to invade Cambodia had been rebuffed repeatedly by the White House over concerns about the political fallout. Abrams and the brass at MACV knew the coup presented their last opportunity to shut down NVA supply lines from Cambodia before the Vietnamization of the war transferred command of military operations to the ARVN. In their minds, the entire U.S. investment in the war would be lost without intervention in Cambodia and defense of Nol's friendly regime in Phnom Penh. But commanders had to act fast before the political winds in Washington shifted and stifled the U.S. involvement in any escalation of the war.

With President Nixon's approval, a secret bombing campaign and covert special operations had been underway for over a year in Cambodia. Harding saw a B-52 strike along the border with Cambodia while on patrol. STABS had also been secretly operating in Cambodia by inserting Navy Seal Teams. Scuttlebutt claimed the Seals had captured a Chinese General enroute to an NVA base in Cambodia.

But MACV commanders knew special ops and bombing NVA positions in Cambodia were not going to eliminate their cleverly hidden underground arms depots or eliminate the COSVN headquarters.

They did not realize at the time how right they were. In one of the most significant intelligence failures of the war, the complex of massive enemy bases, rice stores, hospitals, livestock farms, arms caches, mess halls and kitchens hidden in the triple canopy jungle of the Cambodia forest was grossly underestimated.

Desperation was setting in at MACV. By mid-April, it was apparent to Abrams that NVA troops were rolling over Nol's forces and nearing Phnom Penh. Lon

---

[15] *The Cambodian Incursion, Brigadier General Tran Dinh Tho, ARVN, Maclean, VA, 1978, page 20.*

Nol was frantic for U.S. help while the White House dithered on a decision. On April 17th, MACV, with help from the CIA, transferred 6,000 captured AK-47 rifles to Nol's forces, as Agent Gentry had promised.

President Nixon finally gave the green light to the invasion when he learned that NVA troops were 20 miles from Phnom Penh. Combined U.S./ARVN operation and prepositioned forces began the invasion at the end of April. 50,000 ARVN soldiers and 30,000 U.S. troops participated in the largest and most significant operation of the war. 36 B-52s bombarded suspected NVA troop concentrations with 500-pound bombs. The NVA never anticipated an operation of this size at this point in the war, when political support in the U.S. was waning.

The offensive consisted of three main thrusts. The main attack, named Toan Thang, hit the NVA in the Parrot's Beak and Fishhook regions. The Binh Tay operation struck the enemy across the border from Pleiku. 10 STABs participated in the Cuu Long operation conducted by the ARVN up the Mekong toward Phnom Penh to help Nol's Khmer regime reclaim control of the river[16].

Nixon waited two days after the start of the invasion to announce it. As planned, some NVA troops had moved to the north and west to avoid getting trapped. General Tran held back a security force to defend the massive underground weapons caches and depots hidden away in the triple canopy jungles a few miles from the border. Bunkers dug into the hillsides, defended the largest caches and ensured that any assault by U.S. infantry would result in a high casualty count, which would harm Nixon politically.

Too much effort had gone into digging out the house-size underground caverns and filling them with rockets, mortars, rifles, B-40s, recoilless rifles, ammunition and hand grenades to surrender them without a fight. Area 352, a depot nicknamed The City, covered three square miles and included a 500-bed hospital, lumber yards, 18 mess halls, 500 log-covered bunkers, pig and chicken farms, truck repair facilities, and 38 tons of rice.[17]

A ten-foot-wide bamboo road hid under the triple canopy and extended for miles through Cambodia, linking the truck roads from Laos to arms depots and bases further south. The bamboo was split and laid perpendicularly to the direction of travel and lapped over the adjacent half to hold it in place. Troops and porters

---

[16] Nixon's Cambodian Incursion, James H. Willbanks, History.net, May 2020.
[17] Nixon's Cambodian Invasion, James Willbanks, History.net, May 2020.

walked their bicycles, carts and other conveyances full of weapons down the bamboo road to General Tran's depots along the border. One cache had 400 disassembled bicycles stored underground.

General Tran thought he was ready for the incursion. But NVA commanders had underestimated the scope of the operation, which was the largest of the war.

In-Country R&R

With the infiltration of NVA across the Grand Canal all but halted for the time being by the Cambodian invasion, Commander Perkins gave a few trusted boat crews unofficial, in-country R&R, short for rest and recreation. Harding came off patrol in early May to be told by Lt. Schmidt that his crew had orders to Nha Be to pick up recreational equipment for the squadron. They were flying to Saigon on a Chinook helicopter immediately but had three days to get to Nha Be, which was a cab ride from the city.

"What do we do in Saigon for three days?" Harding asked Schmidt.

"Stay out of trouble," Schmidt said. "Stay together and keep your orders with you in case you get stopped by the Military Police. One of you will need to get on a boat we hired to bring exercise equipment back upriver. Once it arrives here, we'll take it to Phuoc Xuyen."

Harding and his crew were ferried to a landing zone near An Long to board the Chinook to Tan Son Nhut, with little time to gather more than a change of clothes. Harding had only ten dollars in Military Payment Certificates, also known as script, and no time to draw more.

There was no plan for the three-day adventure in Saigon. After landing in Tan Son Nhut, Rizzinato suggested they find a bar in the former French Quarter. He said it was home to some embassies and a higher-class location than The President Hotel, an infamous high-rise brothel that was the usual home for GI excursions.

They took a cab to old Saigon, where the cab driver dropped them off in front of the Paris Club. "Why not?" Harding thought to himself.

Harding noticed that Rizzinato paid the cab driver in cash instead of piasters or script. Cash was more valuable to locals than the military script, which was periodically reissued. Anyone holding old script had to turn it in in exchange for the new issue since the old script became worthless. Already, it seemed that Rizzinato knew all the ropes for these clandestine R&R excursions.

They entered the club and found it virtually empty except for Harding's crew, a bartender, and the female hostesses. A young boy who spoke some English was there to run errands and watch the door for MP patrols. They had orders in hand, so the crews were okay to be out and about until the 10:00 PM curfew when the MPs made their rounds.

It was already 8:00 PM. They ordered fried rice for dinner. The other crew members started drinking "33" beer, the most famous Vietnamese beer among GIs. Harding had been abstaining since he started patrolling and still wasn't drinking. Besides, he was so tired a couple of beers would put him to sleep. He asked the young boy about coffee. The kid eagerly retrieved a cup of instant coffee from behind the bar.

The girls were gathered at a table just across from where the crew was sitting, occasionally chatting with Harding and his crew. Around 9:30, the boy came in to tell everyone the MPs were coming. Two girls gathered up the STAB crew and took them upstairs to hide in the hall on the second floor. The others moved to the back of the bar to avoid having to chat with the MPs and prolong their visit.

It was a game. The MPs knew there were likely to be GIs in the building but made no effort to root them out other than the perfunctory stop. As soon as they were gone, the boy came upstairs to let them know the coast was clear.

It was getting late, and the girls did not want to be up all night, so they each selected a crew member to take to bed. Harding had his eye on one girl, who introduced herself as Cara. He was delighted when she chose him. Normally, there would be more flirting, chit-chat, and negotiation before going off to bed, but none of the STAB crew had much money. So, they hung back until the girls realized they were the only options for the night.

They went into a small room upstairs. Harding told Cara he only had ten dollars. She said that was okay. Harding could not believe how beautiful she was with a perfectly proportioned body. Harding had not had sex for months, not since the Philippines, so it was briefer than he would have liked. Afterward, he put his arm around her and pulled her over to rest her head on his shoulder and fell asleep seconds later.

He awoke in the middle of the night. Unexpectedly, her head was still on his shoulder. He began rubbing her back, hoping she would awaken and have sex with him again, but she woke up and got out of bed.

"Where are you going?" he asked.

"I have to sleep, and you are out of money," she responded.

"Are you going to be here tonight if I come back?"

"Yes, but get here before 8:00 if you want me. I will wait that long, but no longer. You will have more money?" she asked.

"Of course," Harding assured her, although he had no idea where he would get it. He had given her his last penny.

"Okay, I will be here for you," she smiled. "Good night."

Harding was hooked. This woman was so pretty and sweet in a way, not what he expected from a prostitute. He had no regrets about shacking up with a prostitute since death could be waiting for him back on the canal.

Breakfast in Saigon

The crew awoke and assembled in the bar at 8:00 AM. Harding, who was nominally in charge, was relieved he did not have to gather them up. Since there was no food service at the Paris Club in the morning, Rizzinato suggested they catch a cab over to The President Hotel for breakfast. They could also check in there for the next two nights.

After arriving, they went to the restaurant and beer garden at the top of the hotel. Harding needed to figure out how to get some Vietnamese piasters.

Rizzinato said, "No problem. We'll go to the U.S. Exchange in Cholon and buy two cartons of cigarettes for each of us. Then, we will sell them on the black market. I will front you the money. That should net you about $10 dollars. We can also stop by the black market in Cholon if you want to sell your camera."

Harding wondered how Rizinatto had acquired all these Saigon street smarts. He was amazing. How did he know about the black market? Harding had no intention of selling his camera, but it would be worth it for another night with Cara. He wasn't using the camera much anyway because of the inclement weather, and there were few opportunities to take photographs at night.

The black market in Cholon was bustling with street stalls selling electronics, food, and other American goods. Harding found a Chinese woman who offered him 50,000 piasters for his Yashica camera. In U.S. dollars, she was paying about what he had bought for in the PX a year earlier. He was set for the remainder of the visit to Saigon.

The crew headed back to the President to hang out in the rooftop beer garden. Harding was going back to the Paris Club that night but would leave the orders to Nha Be with Rizzinato. He planned to meet the crew back at the President the following day, after which they would head to Nha Be. The likelihood that the MPs were going to stop him was remote since he would be taking a cab over to the Paris Club.

He arrived at the club around 6:00 PM. He was early, but he did not want to miss his rendezvous with Cara. Only the boy and the bartender were present. He ordered fried rice and spring rolls. The boy made instant coffee for him.

Cara arrived with three other girls just before 7:00. She smiled when she saw him, and they found a table at the back of the bar. Harding was mesmerized by her beautiful almond eyes. He wanted to learn more about her life.

She told him the story of how she had been orphaned when she was 12. Her mother taught school, and her father was a police officer in Can Tho.

The Viet Minh were sent South in the early 1960s to destabilize the Diem government. Two VC cadre members had approached Cara's father one day and told him to quit his job with the government. He could not afford to quit but knew the Viet Minh had been murdering government officials and schoolteachers as part of a strategy to undermine the Diem regime. So, he started accompanying Cara's mother home from the Catholic school, where she taught arithmetic. Cara often accompanied them, but on this day, she had left before them because her mother had a faculty meeting.

At a bus stop near Can Tho, the two cadre members with machetes got on the bus and grabbed her father. They dragged him off the bus and told the bus driver to wait for them. Her mother followed, pleading for them to let him go. The first machete blow broke her clavicle, and she fell to the ground. The two VC soldiers proceeded to hack both of them to death, while others on the bus watched in horror.

Cara's aunt had shielded her from the gruesome details, but Cara sought out witnesses, hoping to be able to find out who murdered her parents and turn them over to the police. Cara told Harding that the brutal murder of her parents made her fiercely anti-communist. But she was also very afraid.

She had moved in with her aunt after the murder of her parents. Uncle Bao wanted Cara to help support the family, so she quit school and went to work in her uncle's print shop. Three years after she went to work in the shop, she found a smeared flyer in the trash promoting the Viet Cong and criticizing President Diem as an agent for U.S. imperialism. It had been printed in the shop, so she confronted her uncle, who told her he had been threatened by the VC and had to run a few print jobs for them at night. He said if she knew what was best for her, she would never tell anyone, especially her aunt.

Cara was stunned. How could her uncle work for the killers of her parents? She could not even trust her own uncle. She began planning her escape from Can Tho, fearing the Viet Cong might kidnap her.

Her mother had taught her to sew. She knew there were opportunities for seamstress work in Saigon. Two weeks after finding the flyer, she ran away to Saigon and began working as a seamstress sewing military uniforms. The pay was bad and her living conditions terrible, but at least she felt safer. When she turned 19, she went to work in the club with one of her girlfriends. The pay was much better, and she felt much safer. She made friends with other girls in the club and with the Military Police, who patrolled the district.

Harding learned from reading years later that, under orders from Ho Chí Minh, VC cadres murdered 4,000 government workers and officials supporting the Diem regime every year in the early sixties[18]

School teachers, like Cara's mother, were among their targets. The Diem regime developed the "strategic hamlet" program as a response. It was designed to herd the public into fortified impoundments, sequester, and protect them from the Viet Minh's terror campaign. But the strategic hamlet initiative was rejected by the population and failed miserably. The hamlets were too much like prison. Finally, the Viet Minh quit their murderous campaign after discovering it was alienating the civilian population from the communist cause. The strategic hamlets were abandoned.

The conversation eventually shifted to the events of the day and whether or not Harding had more money. He assured Cara that he had more money, so she took him upstairs for the night. He was enjoying her company and was smitten. He could not believe he had fallen in love, at least temporarily, with a prostitute in Saigon. It was a brief respite from the grind of patrolling the Grand Canal and the specter of death that hung over his life.

The following morning, Cara woke him. He wanted to have sex with her one last time, but she said she had to go. He gave her 15 dollars, which was a handsome sum under the circumstances, and asked if he could write to her.

"No, there are too many VC sympathizers, even among the girls," Cara said. "VC agents occasionally ask them about the Military Police and want us to get

---

[18] Stanley Karnow, Vietnam, A History, 1983, page 238.

information from the diplomats and military officers we meet here. I do not want them coming after me."

Harding took the notepad out of his breast pocket and wrote down his Fleet Post Office address, and his name, Joshua Lee Harding, in blue ink, tore out the page and handed it to her.

"Please write to me and let me know how you are doing. If you are going to work somewhere else, write to me, so I know where to find you. If I get back to Saigon, I want to see you again."

He kissed her forehead. She smiled and touched his cheek with her hand, then left without looking back. He fell back on the bed, staring at the ceiling. There was nothing more he could do. He had already missed the time he was supposed to meet up with his crew at The President Hotel, so he pulled himself up, got dressed, and caught a cab.

After rendezvousing with his crew, they arrived in Nha Be with their orders for recreation equipment, which included a set of weights and an exercise bench. The base quartermaster had arranged for a little river freighter to take the equipment upriver to the Benewah. Boatswain's Mate Carter volunteered to accompany the equipment and boarded the freighter. Harding wondered if he should have a weapon, but Carter didn't seem to care. Harding and the rest of the crew took a chopper back to the Benewah that afternoon.

June 1st, Shakey's Hill

Corporal Buck Newsom jumped off the Chinook with his M-16, pack, and field radio and ran through the dust to a berm, shielding him from the helicopter wash. He had landed on Shakey's Hill, a fire support base 107 miles north of Saigon and 4 miles inside the Cambodian border, to relieve 7th Cavalry units, who had taken the hill at the start of the invasion.

A 15,000-pound bomb with a daisy-cutter fuse had cleared a 260-foot-wide base atop the hill on May 1st. Bravo Company platoons landed on the hill to secure it with M102 howitzers to provide fire support to ARVN and U.S. forces attacking NVA sanctuaries around the Fishhook region.

From Shakey's Hill, search and destroy teams conducted sweeps around the hill looking for weapons caches. Within two weeks of landing on Shakey's Hill, they uncovered 130 tons of weapons and ammunition buried in massive underground caverns dug into the sides of the hill[19]. The North Vietnamese and Viet Cong were the masters of unground infrastructure.

Shakey's Hill was named for Chris Albert Keffalos, the point man for a platoon from the 7th Cavalry Regiment, who was killed while clearing the hill of NVA security forces guarding massive arms caches.

Newsom had been on R&R in Hawaii when the invasion started in May, returning just in time to deploy with his unit to a staging area near the border. While in Hawaii, he had seen TV news reports of the protests on college campuses. In one of life's great ironies, a TV report featured his college roommate slugging the leader of a protest at the University of Georgia's student union.

The fighting around Shakey's Hill was fierce at times. One Go Devil platoon landed on Shakey's Hill with 27 soldiers on May 1st. On June 1st, when they were

---

[19] 9th Infantry Division Newspaper, The Go Devil, Vol. 2, No. 13, June 28, 1970.

rotated out of combat, only 12 were left to get on the Chinook to fly back to their base in South Vietnam.

While most NVA troops had moved to the north and west to avoid the U.S. and ARVN troop deployment, NVA security forces remained to guard massive underground caches, hospitals, and rice stores serving NVA troops assembling for the final assault on South Vietnam.

Newsom's platoon and combat engineers were still encountering stiff resistance in June when they ventured off Shakey's Hill, especially when approaching an area to the southwest. Then, while standing guard on top of the hill one afternoon in early June, Newsom radioed to command that a dust trail was rising out of the forest canopy about a mile to the west, headed in a southerly direction. Reconnaissance patrols confirmed 150 NVA troops entering the area. The Go Devil's commander on Shakey's Hill radioed 1st Cavalry Command to inform them of the coordinates of the troop concentration and the resistance his platoons were encountering.

Two days later, Newsom and three others from his platoon watched as B-52s delivered dozens of 500-pound bombs on those coordinates, which turned out to be a primary arms cache and staging area.

A sweep the following day found a huge swath of the jungle canopy obliterated and cratered by the bombs, unearthing more massive caches of weapons. Along with dozens of dead NVA soldiers and support personnel, 120 enemy combatants were found wandering around the area like zombies. Some had blood running from their ears. They were suffering brain damage inflicted by the concussive impacts and shock waves from the bombing. Only a few were in uniform.

A high-ranking uniformed officer was impaled on a tree branch beside a bomb crater. Engineers cut the limb off the tree, and his body fell to the ground with a thump. A captured NVA officer was brought to the scene to identify him. The South Vietnamese liaison officer gave them the news.

"He say, it General Tran, commander of the base."

Denouement

Enemy infiltration across the Grand Canal had been shut down since the Cambodian invasion and remained that way well into June. There were a few incidents with local Viet Cong, but no major ambushes or encounters with NVA troops, like the ambush executed by Tran's sapper squad. Tran was dead, and his troops were displaced from their border sanctuaries, so infiltration from across the Plain of Reeds and Grand Canal halted while the ARVN and U.S. Army conducted sweeps of southeastern Cambodian provinces.

The NVA's attacks on Lon Nol's Cambodian forces had carried them to the outskirts of Phnom Penh, underscoring the weakness of Cambodia's defenses. Nol's army was saved this time by ARVN forces attacks from the east and south.

The Cambodian invasion stirred up massive anti-war protests in the U.S. Harding was sitting in the mess on the Benewah in early June, reading an old Newsweek published early in May, when he came across the story about the four Kent State students killed and nine others wounded by the National Guard. According to the article, protests against the Cambodian invasion had spread rapidly across college campuses. Inexplicably, National Guard troops opened fire on student protesters at Kent State. The picture of a young woman crying over the body of one of the dead students floored Harding. Another picture showed National Guard troops holding bayoneted rifles in the throats of protesters.

"Why weren't we told about this event?" he wondered. He knew the answer as soon as he asked himself the question. He felt the rug had been pulled out from under him. "Was he now going to be perceived as a mortal enemy of his own generation?"

Action along the canal had diminished significantly since the Cambodian invasion. After three weeks without combat events, boat crews became more casual on their patrols. But danger still lurked in the darkness. One night, all the boats were lined up 50 yards apart on the same side of the river close to the ATSB at Phuoc Xuyen. Water in the canal was low during the dry season, so there was no way to see over the steeper northern bank, which was four or five feet above the waterline.

Around 10:00 PM, a loud explosion interrupted the quiet night. Harding tried to raise the 217 boat to find out what was happening. For some reason, as close as they were, he got no response. Flares from their boat lit the landscape.

Finally, the 217 boat captain radioed that an RPG had been fired at them. It had missed and hit the bank close to Harding's boat. When the boats were lined up on the same side of the river, their backside was no longer covered. It was a one-round pot shot, but it revealed that the VC were still lurking in the dark, waiting for an opportunity to ambush gunboats.

Harding wondered how many of them would have been killed if Commander Perkins had not sent two boats to each guard post, one on each bank to cover the backsides. One boat alone along the bank of an enemy infiltration route was a sitting duck for sapper squads.

After the attack, Chief Stokes, who was the patrol captain on the 217 boat that night, refused to go out on patrol again. He was eligible for retirement and wanted to live to see it. He applied for retirement and left the Squadron shortly afterward.

STABS were not standing down, but their operations were changing as the Vietnamization of the war effort advanced. In early July, Commander Perkins announced that the Squadron would be broken in two. Nine boat crews, who had been in the country longer, were going to Nha Be to patrol the Long Tau shipping channel into Saigon. The VC had been taking shots at the old World War II Liberty ships steaming up the river to deliver military supplies for the war effort. Ten boats were going to Dong Tam to continue combat operations with the South Vietnamese, a much riskier operation than Nha Be.

Harding's crew was assigned to the Nha Be operation. After seven months of combat operations, he felt like his half of the squadron was going on vacation compared to the boats assigned to Dong Tam. He didn't like it, but he was relieved that sapper squads were unlikely to be hunting him while on patrol in Nha Be. He was also tired from relentless nighttime patrolling. Since he would be near Saigon, he thought about visiting Cara again, so he didn't volunteer for the Dong Tam assignment.

Harding's assessment was right; the U.S. was in the process of withdrawing from the war. President Nixon called it "Vietnamization" as if the Vietnamese cared enough to assume the burden. Harding's experience suggested that the Vietnamese could not win the war alone, and everyone knew it. There were ardent Vietnamese commanders and troops committed to defeating the communists, but the NVA and VC seemed far more motivated than the passive Vietnamese he had met.

General Abrams, commander of MACV in Saigon, was fighting a face-saving, rearguard operation that seemed pointless at times, especially since it was still costing young men their lives. He did his best under the circumstances, but the die was cast. The U.S. was pulling out, and that retreat was about to accelerate.

Leaving the Mekong River and the boondocks around the Grand Canal was bittersweet for Harding. He relished the challenge of combat patrols. He had theorized that the ever-present risk of ambush while on patrol was manageable if he stayed on his toes and awake at night. He had gone from thinking that he was going to die to realizing that he would survive if he kept his wits about him. Yes, there was always the risk of a pot shot, sniper round, or RPG ambush, but that risk was acceptable to him. He hated sitting around trying to find something useful to do.

Patrolling on his powerful Strike Assault Boat was what he enjoyed the most. Patrolling at night was a game of survival. To watch a line of NVA soldiers in the distance through the eerie yellow light of the Starlight scope and calling for air support had a seductive appeal to him that he could not quite understand.

Although it was initially frightening, patrolling at night had become routine. The degree to which he had stifled fear and adjusted to it was revealed in April when a reporter for the military newspaper Stars and Stripes rode along on patrol. The reporter picked up an M-16 when darkness fell and flinched at every little sound as if he was near panic. Harding had to take the M-16 away from him for fear he would open fire indiscriminately.

Many events had occurred during the squadron's operation on the Grand Canal, which he hoped would not be lost and forgotten.

There was the pagoda that the VC used as cover to fire on a STAB patrol, after which the pagoda mysteriously burned to the ground. ARVN troops later found weapons cached under its ruins. The joke around the squadron about destroying a sacred site was: "What pagoda?"

Then, the interdiction of the NVA entertainment troop and the female singer's diary revealed her journey down the Ho Chí Minh Trail. Her pack, along with her clothes, bras and guitar, were left in their retreat after the troupe had been shot trying to cross the canal.

A Chinese machine gun was recovered after another NVA crossing was stopped on the outskirts of Phuoc Xuyen by PBRs and STABs. There was Harding's mysterious trip into Cambodia to ferry the Cambodian naval officer downriver for reasons that were never revealed to him. In retrospect, he assumed it was to plan the Cambodian invasion or part of some sort of reward for the officer's help freeing Westy.

Then there was the day when hundreds of bodies floated by the Benewah from the massacres by Lon Nol's forces. And most prominent of all, those in the Squadron killed and wounded in action, who would likely be forgotten by all but their families and their buddies in the squadron.

Harding wished he had a better picture of the events swirling around their operations on the Grand Canal. Occasionally, a Stars and Stripes Newspaper covering military events during the war could be found in the mess. But most of the news about the war came from scuttlebutt. There were no briefings, even for boat captains, about the military engagements around their operations, like the Cambodian invasion in which they participated. Some of the operations were classified and only revealed years later.

According to Newsweek magazine, the Cambodian invasion was seen by the public and protesters back home as an escalation of the war. Driving the NVA out of Cambodia for good was never the objective, since Nixon announced on May 7th that U.S. forces would withdraw by June 30th. Nixon claimed the invasion was needed to buy more time for the Vietnamization of the war effort, which was true, but it was also necessary to stop the NVA from taking control of Phnom Penh and most of Cambodia.

A few weeks later, in Nha Be, Harding read a report in which MACV in Saigon claimed that the incursion had resulted in the capture of "more than

22,800 individual and 2,500 crew-served weapons and more than 1,700 tons of ammunition and 680 tons of rice, as well as quantities of miscellaneous supplies."[20] He thought the bounty was probably exaggerated, just like enemy casualty counts, but he was wrong.

The Cambodian invasion was one of the most successful military operations of the war. However, the fallout contributed to South Vietnam's eventual demise. Violent protests erupted across the nation. 30 ROTC buildings were torched across college campuses. 4 million students staged a walkout at 450 college campuses and high schools across the U.S.

The Cambodian invasion sacrificed 344 more lives and wounded another 1,600 U.S. service members. It did nothing to stop the communists in their quest for victory. The success of the ARVN in taking down NVA troops in Cambodia was used to claim they were ready for Vietnamization, which was an illusion. Without U.S. air support and planning, the ARVN would have never gotten to first base. U.S. forces would soon be prohibited from supporting combat operations in another country without prior Congressional approval.

Eventually, the political reaction to the Cambodian invasion led to the passage of the War Powers Act, curtailing presidential authority to conduct armed aggression without congressional approval.

Many events back home, like the massive war protests and the Apollo missions to the moon, passed into history unnoticed by veterans in the backcountry of Vietnam. They were shielded from the protests erupting on college campuses. The animus against Vietnam veterans grew with each fiery protest and the military's response to put down rioters. Many veterans would be ambushed by this hostility upon their return home. Instead of being welcomed home, they faced indifference, disdain, and stigma as drug-addled ne'er-do-wells, especially when their lives went off the tracks.

Harding now began to wonder if the 50,000 dead and 150,000 wounded were cannon fodder for politicians and military brass. Turning the war over to the Vietnamese was admitting defeat. If that is what the Vietnamese wanted, fine, but don't sacrifice any more U.S. in the process. He thought the U.S. should be

---

[20] *MACV: The Years of Withdrawal, 1968–1973, page 302.*

all in to win for good, moral reasons, or the lives of young Americans should not be sacrificed to the whims of an elite political class to help them save face and recover from a series of bad decisions.

Despite his misgivings about the conduct of the Vietnam War, Harding committed to doing his best every day because those were the values his dad taught him.

Long Tau

After leaving the Mekong, Harding's crews patrolled the Long Tau shipping channel through the Rung Sat Special Zone, which Agent Orange had totally denuded. Since the boat had no canopy or cover, the sun took its toll on fair-skinned sailors like Harding. To cool off, when the tide came in, and the water seemed clean and clear, Harding stripped to his skivvies and took daily swims from the back of his gunboat. He had not considered the pollution coming downriver out of Saigon or the potential impacts of Agent Orange leaching out of the nearby soil. Sores developed on his hands, which a corpsman attributed to sun exposure, but in retrospect, Harding would wonder if Agent Orange caused it. The sores and sea snakes finally convinced him to stay out of the cooling waters.

At the end of October, three months of patrolling the Long Tau in Nha Be ended. The Squadron reunited in Saigon and prepared to ship out the first week of November. Only one hostile fire event occurred during the three months in Nha Be. The squadron reassembled at the Annapolis barracks on Plantation Road in Saigon for a few days of processing to await a flight back to the States.

Harding took the opportunity to cab over to the Paris Club to see if he could find Cara and say goodbye. He knew finding her was probably a long shot, but seeing her again would be worth the trip, even if he was out of bounds. He just wanted to see her again, say goodbye, and thank her for the brief respite from the grind of war she gave him. Perhaps she would write to him in the States.

He arrived at the club late in the afternoon and asked the cab driver to wait. If Cara wasn't there, he would return to the Annapolis barracks quickly. The club was open but vacant, except for the young boy and bartender.

Harding asked the boy about Cara.

"Oh," he said. "She leave club long time ago. Went to work for MPs." The bartender looked over, said nothing, but just shook his head. "She get pregnant," the boy continued. Harding gave him a dollar and took the cab back to the *Annapolis*.

Harding left Saigon on November 5, 1970, after spending over 10 months in-country with **STABRON 20**. The entire squadron flew home in their fatigues wearing their black berets. Even without family and friends to greet them, walking down the gangway to touch American soil again was a proud moment. Just like those fighter pilots and tank jockeys in World War II who left their machines, he regretted that he would never again be in command of a 650-horsepower gunboat.

STAB crews spent almost two months at Treasure Island in California waiting for reassignment. Harding turned down an opportunity to be evaluated for the Officer Candidate program because it required a 6-year re-enlistment. He received the Navy Commendation medal for his diligence, readiness, and superior performance as boat captain of Strike Assault Boat 210. The citation said he had been calm in combat. Commander Perkins received the Bronze Star with a V for "valor." Harding was mystified, since he had never seen him on patrol, but a lot went on that was never shared, so Perkins may have done some things Harding never heard about.

He separated from the Navy a year later after a stint at the naval air station in Pensacola, Florida. All the service branches were reducing their forces as the U.S. pulled out of Vietnam, so he got out three months early. During his last months in the service, Harding read the Pentagon Papers, Daniel Ellsberg's leaked study about the backroom deliberations, and classified studies that revealed the true story about the war effort. The public had been deceived about the war from the beginning, and only President Kennedy seemed to develop an understanding of the situation just before his assassination, contrary to what his intelligence agencies had told him. The inflated casualty counts and the likely presence of a spy at MACV in Saigon were revealed in the Pentagon Papers.

When Harding entered the service, he thought the government was honest, humane, and truthful. Now, he wasn't so sure. It was not above lying to the public to enable support for the mission and benefits to a political class that went beyond the government's legitimate objectives. The Pentagon Papers and his own experience confirmed that.

The Beginning of the End

The Vietnamization of the war, the drawdown of U.S. forces, and the transfer of combat operations to the Vietnamese were moving at a rapid pace by the end of 1970. Within two years, only advisors, support personnel, and air assets remained in the country to support the Vietnamese military.

The performance of ARVN forces, who were supposed to take command of the war, was spotty. One of the first signs that the South's fate was sealed showed its face shortly after STABRON 20 left Vietnam. On the heels of the successful disruption of NVA supply lines during the Cambodian invasion, General Creighton Abrams, commander of MACV in Saigon, lobbied hard for an invasion into Laos to undermine logistics and supply lines to the NVA in the northern provinces of South Vietnam.[21] The combat operations would have to be executed exclusively by ARVN forces with some air support from the U.S.

In early February 1971, South Vietnam's best Airborne, Marine and Infantry units entered Laos under the command of Lt. Gen. Hoang Xuan Lam. Operation Lam Son 719 was supposed to take Tchepone, Loas, a logistical hub along the Ho Chí Minh Trail about 25 miles from the Vietnamese border.[22]

The attack proved to be a disaster, revealing the timidity and incompetence of South Vietnamese commanders. Disorganization afflicted the South Vietnamese command. ARVN forces dilly-dallied and lost all momentum, giving the NVA time to assemble armored assets and surround South Vietnam's fire bases. Meanwhile, Abrams was extorting his South Vietnamese counterparts while giving glowing reports about the operation to the Joint Chiefs in Washington. By March 9th, mounting casualties and the lack of progress prompted President

---

[21] Brigadier General John D. Howard, This General Challenged the President and Saved Lives, Military Times, November 2, 2017.
[22] Ibid.

Nguyen Văn Thieu to withdraw his forces, a move described as "losing his nerve."[23] Abrams had egg on his face and was almost relieved of command.

Nonetheless, in April 1971, President Nixon went on television, touting the Lam Son 710 invasion as demonstrating the success of the Vietnamization of the war, which was another lie foisted on the public.

The Lam Son experience convinced the North that it could win a head-to-head confrontation with the South's forces, even with U.S. air support. Planning for the 1972 Easter Offensive began. On March 30, 1972, using heavy weapons never seen below the DMZ, the Offensive was launched, quickly overrunning ARVN forces, impeded only by valiant South Vietnamese Marines. A few days later, NVA forces stormed out of Cambodian sanctuaries and attacked An Loc, about 60 miles from Saigon.[24]

Only 50,000 U.S. troops remained in South Vietnam in support positions along with special forces. Troops secured the U.S. airbases in Danang and Biên Hòa, which were necessary to support the South's operations. In response to the North's Easter Offensive, Nixon ramped up air support and mined North Vietnam's harbors. The increased air support and intelligence from the U.S. enabled the South to hold on, but the poor leadership demonstrated during the Lam Son operation still afflicted the ARVN's efforts. None of the incompetent, politically connected generals had been replaced.

In May, South Vietnamese soldiers in I Corps abandoned the city of Quang Trí and fled south in panic."[25] The NVA occupied Quang Trí City after the ARVN retreat. Hundreds of civilians died from indiscriminate shelling by the NVA, one of many such massacres by the communists that were greater than the My Lai massacre but hardly noticed by the media.

Abrams appealed for and received authorization for the ramped-up bombing of NVA positions to stave off the North's advances.

Finally, President Thieu replaced General Lam with the capable Lt. Gen. Ngô Quang Truong, which boosted the morale of the South's forces aided by air

---

[23] Ibid.
[24] Ibid.
[25] Ibid.

support and U.S. Navy guns off the coast. The NVA's Easter Offensive ground to a halt in June 1972 under heavy bombing and effective reorganization of ARVN commanders[26]. The NVA's loss of troops and heavy weapons was significant. Stopping the Easter Offensive had one benefit. It helped Henry Kissinger, Nixon's National Security Advisor, establish a better negotiating position with the North during their Paris talks. The South was holding on, but not for long.

[26] Ibid.

Shattered Dreams

Harding separated from the Navy in November 1971 and moved back to Tennessee to start classes at the State University in January. The country's turmoil and the specter of revolution promoted by war protesters led him to major in political science, even though his previous major had been agriculture.

Without a TV or source for news other than an occasional newspaper, the events unfolding in South Vietnam were lost on Harding.

He began his orientation for the Winter Quarter with a meeting with Dr. Jones, his faculty advisor.

"You look older than most of my students," Jones said as the meeting started.

"I just got out of the service," Harding replied.

"Were you in Vietnam?".

"Yes," Harding replied.

"I see. Well, here are the courses I am going to assign to you. Poly Science 101, Spanish 101 and Statistics. That's the course we use to weed people out."

Harding left the meeting not particularly upset or concerned; he was just disappointed at his faculty advisor's unfriendly attitude.

He had bought a house trailer and moved into it with a cousin who paid rent and covered the cost of the rental slot. 16 months in the combat zone with combat pay and nowhere to spend it enabled him to save several thousand dollars, which he had budgeted out for the next two years in a plan to get him through his last two years of college. His goal was to get a master's degree. The GI Bill's college benefits were a great help but not enough to cover all his expenses, so he ate hard-boiled eggs for most of his meals since they were only 29 cents a dozen.

Studying was proving to be a challenge. Learning to learn again required exercising the brain in ways that he had not done for four years. Concentrating was difficult. Nevertheless, he was making Bs when calamity struck.

During a Spanish midterm, his right hand began shaking uncontrollably, and he could not concentrate or write. He had studied and felt prepared, but now he was in a cold sweat. He had abstained from drinking alcohol since school started, so it wasn't that.

"What is happening to me?" he wondered.

Unable to write or concentrate, he got up and gave the incomplete exam to the professor, a Cuban woman who frowned as he said, "I don't feel well and have to go outside."

"You can't come back in," she said.

Harding ran outside into the fresh air. He was going to get an "F" on the test, and that would result in failing the course, which would kill his college plans and disqualify him for GI Bill benefits.

The following day, he went to the campus clinic. The doctor said it might be depression and gave him a prescription for Valium.

It was clear that his Spanish professor was not going to allow him to retake the test, so he withdrew from school entirely to avoid getting the F on this record and losing GI Bill college funding.

For four years, he had counted the days until his discharge so he could go back to college. Those dreams and his life plan were shattered now. He lay on the couch, wondering what to do next. How had this happened? He had been calm in combat. He had heard about post-traumatic stress disorder but did not believe it was real, at least not for him. Even after an old friend had told him that he had changed dramatically from the happy-go-lucky person he once knew, Harding denied he suffered from PTSD. Combat had not bothered him. It was the insanity of a politicized U.S. war effort, the sacrifice of lives, the austere living conditions, and the relentless patrolling without sleep that wore him down.

Now, what was he going to do? Suicide was one option, but he knew he could not pull the trigger. He also realized that no one was going to help him. Something a former girlfriend told him kept running through his head: "People love you for your strengths, not your weaknesses." He would have to find a way out of this funk on his own and keep it quiet. He decided to do everything in his power to be well.

He arranged a meeting with Dr. Conrad, a World War II veteran, family friend and veterinarian who had graduated from the University and still had connections there. He urged Harding to go back to school and give it one more try. Dr. Conrad made a call to the University on his behalf. He also noticed that Harding had lost a lot of weight, another symptom of depression. He told Harding to start eating better and get some exercise.

"In a couple of days, I want you to make an appointment with the Dean of Students, explain your situation, ask him to readmit you and help you with the Spanish professor so you can retake the exam," Dr. Conrad said.

Harding had been out of school for a week when he entered Dean Anderson's office. Although the dean seemed to be in a hurry, he had taken just enough time to familiarize himself with Harding's situation.

"I don't know what happened," Harding said. "I guess it was a panic attack. Will you readmit me and ask the Spanish teacher to let me retake the test?"

"No," Dean Anderson responded.

"Please, give me another chance," Harding pleaded.

"No!" was all he said.

"Please, I am a Vietnam veteran trying to get my feet back under me," Harding said, hating to use that excuse, but he was desperate.

Dean Anderson looked at him for a second and said, "Okay, follow me."

They were like magic words. Without any discussion, Dean Anderson reversed himself. Harding thought, "he must have seen this before."

Dean Anderson told his secretary to get Harding re-admitted and to call Ms. Cruz in the Spanish Department. "After I talk with her, you will go to her and ask her to let you retake the mid-term. Good day."

Harding resumed classes the following week. He met with Ms. Cruz, who was reluctant but had been ordered to re-administer the midterm.

While retaking the midterm the following Thursday, Harding realized halfway through the test that it was not the midterm for Spanish 101. It seemed like a higher-level exam for Spanish 102, but he said nothing. Was this Ms. Cruz's way of penalizing Harding for what she considered to be cheating on the exam?

This time, there was no uncontrollable shaking and sweating. He made a "D" on the test even though it was not for his course. It was good enough when averaged with his other grades to get a "C" for the final grade. He finished the quarter with two "B"s and a "C." It was not what he had hoped for, but it was better than failing and dropping out, and he still had GI Bill benefits for college.

During the dark hours of contemplation, lying on the couch in his trailer, he realized that his life had been one of deferred gratifications for so long that he wasn't enjoying it. Not to mention the anger that welled up in him about the sacrifice of so many young lives in a mismanaged, politically directed war. The anger welled up inside him and was bringing him down. He had to let it go.

He also needed to add some adventure to his life and get some exercise, following Dr. Conrad's advice. So, he bought a bicycle to ride to class every day. He threw away the Valium. He also started eating better. The combination of diet and exercise improved his outlook dramatically.

As the quarter progressed, he became increasingly disenchanted with Political Science. While the subject had merits, one professor used his daily lecture to rail against the Vietnam War, Republicans, Richard Nixon, Henry Kissinger, or whatever else popped up in the news that day. It was as if the course had no professional underpinnings.

Harding decided to return to his original major prior to joining the service, which was Agriculture and Animal Husbandry. He grew up on the family's 100-acre farm, not enough land to make a living farming, but enough to raise a herd of cows and keep a couple of horses. Their freezer was never wanting for beef.

After a mediocre performance in his first quarter in school, he had righted his ship sufficiently to make the dean's list for every quarter thereafter. He developed a knack for focusing on the issues that were going to be tested. He graduated with honors two years later despite his weak first quarter. He would never reveal his troubles to anyone outside the family.

Fleeing Saigon

While Harding was trying to get his feet back under him back in the U.S., the South Vietnamese were dealing with the consequences of their ill-fated alliance with the Americans. It was apparent to many South Vietnamese that the war was not going to end well for them, especially if they had aligned themselves with Diem, Thieu and the U.S.

Cara left the Paris Club in June 1970, shortly after discovering she was pregnant. The U.S. Military Police, who visited the club nightly as part of their patrol, had a billet nearby. They liked Cara, so when she announced she was leaving the club, they took up a collection and offered her a job as their housekeeper and assistant cook. Her baby was born March 5, 1971. She named the baby girl Linh. Her father was obviously American.

The MPs were good to Cara. After Linh's birth, some of them helped rock her to sleep while Cara did her chores. She avoided romantic relationships with the MPs, whom she knew would be gone within a few months. She certainly could not afford to have another fatherless child. Still, these were among the happiest days in Cara's life. They would be short-lived.

In December 1972, with the U.S. pull-out imminent just before the MPs closed their billet near the French Quarter in Saigon, Cara fled to Can Tho. Aunt Nguyen Hòa was home when she arrived at her doorstep. Cara had written to her occasionally, but her aunt was not happy with Cara's choices in life and her work as a prostitute, so she stopped corresponding with her. Now, here she was, showing up on her doorstep with a toddler who was not going to be accepted in the Vietnamese community. Under the control of North Vietnam, Amerasian children in the South were called "bui doi," which translates to "the dust of life."

Aunt Hòa knew Cara's uncle would not accept Cara and the child. They were struggling as the U.S. withdrew and the South's economy contracted. Government print jobs evaporated. Cara's Aunt Hòa and her husband Bao knew the Viet Cong and the North would win the war. The last thing they needed was the curse of an

Amerasian child living with them, a sign that a collaborator was in the household. The Nguyens were members of the Hòa sect, people of Chinese descent. The North Vietnamese had a special enmity for the Hòa. Chinese-Vietnamese entrepreneurs owned many of the shops and businesses in the South and were imbued with an independence that defied communist rule.

After tea, Aunt Hòa told Cara to sit while she ran to the print shop to talk to her uncle. She knew she could not push Cara into the streets with little money and a baby, so she conceived a plan that Uncle Bao would accept. She would propose that Cara work in the print shop again in exchange for room and board in the spare room in their house. She knew he would reject that proposal. But he could save face by allowing them to stay a few days until they visited the orphanage in Can Tho.

"One week! That is all," Uncle Bao said. He could not risk having Cara and her child around, given his already shaky relationship with the Viet Cong.

During the week, Aunt Hòa took Cara to the orphanage in Can Tho, which had many fatherless children given up by their destitute mothers. Cara would never willingly give up her child, but the orphanage might be her only option at some point.

As the week progressed, baby Linh, who enjoyed snuggling in the laps of the MPs, crawled into Uncle Bao's lap and went to sleep. Aunt Hòa saw them sitting together. It was as if a special peace had fallen over Uncle Bao, which she had not seen for a while.

Their own children were gone; one son had been killed in the war, another was still fighting in the northern provinces, and a daughter had married and moved to Saigon. There was room in their small house. One week turned into two weeks. Cara started working in the shop. Aunt Hao and Uncle Bao were in love with their toddler niece. Talk about their leaving never came up again.

The Republic of South Vietnam's Final Days

President Nixon was driven to end the U.S. involvement in the war by negotiating a peace deal that would allow the South and its quasi-democratic status to remain intact, which meant negotiating stiff penalties for violating the peace accords. Nixon suspected Henry Kissinger, his national security advisor and chief negotiator, privately just wanted to bring U.S. troops and POWs home without much concern about what the final agreement meant to the fate of the South Vietnamese. Suspicious of Kissinger's goals, Nixon assigned General Alexander Haig to spy on him.

Despite being weakened by his own perils during the Watergate scandal, Nixon wanted a defensible, face-saving peace to end the war. He rejected Kissinger's initial proposed Paris Peace Accords over concerns that they did not require the North to withdraw forces from the South. He also wanted to initiate a bombing campaign if the North violated a cease-fire agreement.

Kissinger maneuvered around Nixon by convincing President Thieu to accept the Paris Peace Accords after promising to punish the North if they violated the Accords. He also told Thieu the U.S. would replace any military hardware and ammunition expended in defense of the South. These were hollow promises, since Kissinger could not force the United States to comply with his verbal assurance to Thieu.

The Paris Peace Accords were signed on January 27, 1973, ending the U.S. involvement in the War. One of the primary benefits to the U.S. was the return of all American POWs and the withdrawal of all U.S. forces except for a few thousand Department of Defense employees. The North was not required to move any of its troops or bases out of the South, which had been a condition of the 1955 armistice.

The accords were the kiss of death for South Vietnam. Kissinger had made secret promises to President Thieu, promising to react militarily if the North violated the accords, but those promises evaporated when the U.S. Congress passed the

Case-Church amendment in August 1973, prohibiting American military action in Southeast Asia without their prior congressional authorization.[27]

Under pressure from the Watergate Scandal and congressional hearings, President Nixon resigned in August 1974. Any personal assurances his administration made to the South Vietnamese scattered like a covey of quail with his departure to retirement in California.

The North was ready for this day. After building up their troop strength and material, the North tested the United States' resolve in December of that year by invading and capturing Phuoc Long Province, just 60 miles from Saigon. For the first time in the history of the war, the North had taken control of an entire province in the South.[28]

In the last face-saving gasp, Nixon's successor, President Gerald Ford, wrote to Congress on January 28, 1975, requesting $300 million for a supplemental appropriation for military aid to South Vietnam and additional funding for Cambodia to fight the Khmer Rouge. By the time Congress got around to denying Ford's request in April, the South was nearing defeat.[29]

The failure of the U.S. to retaliate after the Phuoc Long victory was the North's green light to initiate a full-scale invasion of the South, known as the Spring Offensive of 1975. It advanced much faster than the North anticipated. In March, Thieu's own fickle leadership led to the withdrawal of several ARVN divisions from the northern provinces. Their surrender of the five northern provinces to the North quickly followed the ARVN withdrawal.

Once again, relentless shelling by the communists killed thousands of retreating ARVN soldiers and the trailing civilian population during a panicked retreat along Highway 7 B.[30] By April 1975, Saigon was surrounded, and ARVN forces were running low on ammunition.

---

[27] https://alphahistory.com/vietnamwar/fall-of-south-vietnam/
[28] Tom Glenn, Bitter Memories: The Fall of Saigon, April 1975, (Studies in Intelligence, Vol. 59, No. 4, 2015), page 11.
[29] David Rosenbaum, Defeat for Ford, (New York Times, April 18, 1975), page 1.
[30] Tom Glenn, Bitter Memories: The Fall of Saigon, April 1975, (Studies in Intelligence, Vol. 59, No. 4, 2015), page 11.

With her aunt and uncle, Cara watched President Thieu's television address to the nation on April 21, 1975, at a wealthy friend's house in Can Tho. Thieu lashed out at the U.S. for its treachery and broken promises in his angry speech. He said Henry Kissinger had tricked him into accepting the Paris Peace Accords with promises of continuing support.

Thieu looked straight into the camera and spoke:

"At the time of the [Paris] peace agreement, the United States agreed to replace equipment on a one-by-one basis. But the United States did not keep its word. Is an American's word reliable these days? The United States did not keep its promise to help us fight for freedom, and it was in the same fight that the United States lost 50,000 of its young men ... The United States has not respected its promises. It is inhumane. It is untrustworthy. It is irresponsible ... You ran away and left us to do the job that you could not do."[31]

Then, in the ultimate act of duplicity, Thieu fled South Vietnam with help from the CIA. The NVA drove the final American and ARVN forces out of Saigon at the end of April, 1975. General Dương Văn Minh surrendered on April 30th, ending the war for good.

Cara knew her future was dark since she had worked for the U.S. in Saigon. She feared the vicious Viet Cong, who had murdered her parents, and doubted the NVA would be more merciful.

The Viet Cong had taken control of much of the Mekong Delta before the South's surrender as Thieu's incompetent generals moved troops to the north to fight the incursion of the North's Easter Offensive.

When the South's defeat was imminent, Cara stopped working at the print shop and stayed out of sight. She worked in the garden behind the fence at the house, helping her aunt grow fresh vegetables.

A month after the South's surrender, rumors were spreading that the provisional government was setting up camps for former officers and collaborators with the U.S. forces. The North's original plan had been to execute many of the South Vietnamese military commanders, officers, and government officials. Some were shot in the days immediately after the surrender. But so many in the South would

---

[31] BBC Archives from 21 April 1975 (http://news.bbc.co.uk/onthisday/hi/dates/stories/april/21/newsid_2935000/2935347.stm)

have to be executed, Hanoi's leaders realized that the world would condemn them as a pariah state.

Within weeks, the provisional government began setting up re-education camps to imprison those perceived as a threat to the Hanoi regime. Members of Viet Cong cadres were given lists of citizens and former army officers to track down and take to provincial headquarters for processing and assignment to a camp.

Cara hoped she could escape their scrutiny until the day two Viet Cong soldiers carrying AK-47s showed up at the Nguyen's home. Cara was listed as a collaborator and would have to go to a re-education camp for two or three weeks, they said. They told her to pack a small bag with a change of clothes.

Cara's aunt followed her into the room where Linh was sleeping. Tears streamed down Cara's face as she looked at her napping daughter. She moved over to a table where a small lock box sat and gave it to her aunt. She then took off her necklace with the key to the box and gave it to Aunt Hòa.

"Unlock this after I am gone. Look for the page from the notepad. It has the name of Linh's father on it. Linh may need that someday. Don't lose it."

She picked Linh up, who had been awakened by commotion. With a final hug, she said, "Mother has to go. I will be back in a few days. I love you."

Cara grabbed her bag of clothes and left with the two Viet Cong. She would be confined to a camp outside of Can Tho.

Aunt Hòa was allowed to visit Cara once a week and give her small amounts of food through the wire fence. Initially, she brought Linh until the toddler became so distraught at having to be pulled away at the end of the visit that they thought it best to keep her away, especially after Cara got sick. Three months after entering the re-education camp, Cara died, worn down by her broken heart, hard labor, dysentery, and an untreated respiratory infection that turned into pneumonia.

Family Days

As the war was winding down in Vietnam, Harding was finishing his senior year in the College of Agriculture. His father introduced him to a friend who was an official in the state's Department of Agriculture Farm Service Program. The meeting opened the door for Harding to intern with the state program during the last quarter of his senior year, after which he was offered a job with the Service.

The job was like being a social worker for farmers, helping them with the Department of Agriculture's bureaucracy, crop supports, crop rotation, conservation and managing herds. Most of the farmers knew far more than he did about these matters, but he could tie them into state and federal programs designed to sustain the nation's food supply. He had a state car but was still living at his dad's home until he got his feet on the ground financially.

During his second year working for the State, he got a call from a young woman who was in the process of taking over her father's 800-acre farm. Betsy Barnett had just graduated from nursing school at State University when a heart condition sidelined her father. He was being evaluated by cardiologists at the University Hospital where Betsy worked. She could not afford to give up her career to take over the marginally profitable farm, so she called Harding's office to have him offer her some options.

Betsy's mother died from breast cancer when she was 12, so as her father's health failed, the burden of overseeing the farm fell squarely on her shoulders. Mr. Barnett had a reliable farm hand, Rufus Jefferson, but he was also getting too old to manhandle heavy equipment. There was no one to manage the finances and schedule the big chores. Selling the farm seemed to be the only viable option.

Harding began to make regular visits to Betsy's place after she got off work. Then they began dating, first to discuss farm business over dinner and then to enjoy a few movies together. Harding's hearing loss prevented him from understanding much of the dialogue, but he kept quiet about it.

The Barnett farm was outside Holston City, a small town north of Knoxville, Tennessee, which had been a whistlestop on the southern train line. The fertile land and rolling hills along the Holston River made it an idyllic setting for a farm, even though the finances of running it were challenging.

Josh had been working for the state for about two years when he woke up one morning and realized that no one really cared whether he went to work that day or not. At dinner one night, he told Betsy about his dissatisfaction with the state job and that he was considering moving on if he could find the right opportunity.

Betsy introduced Josh to one of her father's friends, who was the chair of the State Stockgrowers Association. As fate would have it, the Association was considering hiring an executive director to serve as a lobbyist for the group and help grow membership and services. State and federal regulations were ramping up, so the group needed professional management and a lobbyist who understood government programs for farmers. Harding's experience with state regulations and his many contacts among stock growers and state employees made him an attractive candidate. The pay was not that great, and some travel was involved, but Josh thought it had potential, so he gave his notice to the state and was hired shortly thereafter as the first executive director of the State Stockgrowers Association.

Mr. Barnett's heart condition worsened, and he died from complications related to coronary bypass surgery, which had only been partially successful in restoring blood flow to his left ventricle. He never got back on his feet after the surgery, which they knew was high risk. Betsy found him dead in his bed one morning in early March. He had died peacefully in his sleep.

After summoning an ambulance, Betsy called Josh. When he arrived at the house, she ran to him and fell into his arms, crying. She pulled her head back and looked into his teary eyes. That was the moment he realized he loved this woman and had to do everything possible to help her. He would never let her go.

The day after the funeral with the relatives departed, she cooked Josh dinner, and he stayed over. First, it was one night, then two, and then three or four times per week. After a month, he moved in at her invitation. He could not stand to think of her living alone in a big farmhouse in the country.

Josh and Besty married on a Saturday in October 1978 on a hill overlooking the Holston River Valley. It was a small wedding attended by family and close friends.

Betsy's dog, Scotty, stood next to them, looking up at her. As they exchanged vows, he sat there as if he were part of the vows and would not be left out. The wedding picture was classic.

One of the guests at the wedding was Westford Hollins. Josh and Westy exchanged a few letters while he served one year at the Portsmouth Naval Prison in Kittery, Maine, for dereliction of duty. Upon release, Westy worked on offshore oil rigs but struggled to find a home, given the itinerant nature of the job.

Josh invited him to the wedding. Westy drove over with his travel trailer in tow. During his stay, he decided to put down roots in Holston City, close to one of the few friends he had left in the world. Two weeks later, on Josh's recommendation, he found a job working for Holston County, maintaining their trucks and generators.

Eminent Domain

One year after the communists raised North Vietnam's flag in Can Tho, Uncle Bao stormed into the house and found his wife in the kitchen.

"The communists are taking over my print shop! I no longer own it. They handed me this decree and said the shop was needed to advance the goals of the revolution. It says, 'Contributing my shop to the government will confirm my commitment to the revolution.' Today, I met the new manager. I am to work for him. He knows nothing about printing. But he will decide what we print and when. He receives all payments. They will give me a small monthly stipend. They took our son, and now they are taking my business."

The Nguyens had known for several years that a new level of turmoil would be coming to the South after the North victory. They knew communist central planners did not support entrepreneurs, so they had to be prepared as best they could. Their risks were compounded by the animus toward Vietnamese of Chinese descent. At least in the South, where free markets had flourished, they had not been persecuted and had been allowed to run their businesses without much government interference. If the South lost the war, that level of tolerance might end, and the piaster would lose its value. So, Aunt Hòa had been hoarding dollars and using them to buy gold jewelry on the black market. Now, they could use their savings to escape.

By 1977, the Hòa people and others disaffected with communist control had begun fleeing Vietnam by boat. The exodus was an embarrassment to the communist promise of a utopian workers' paradise. Uncle Bao began to hear rumors among his Hòa friends about plans to flee by boat to China, Hong Kong, or Malaysia. But many Vietnamese could not be trusted. He had to be careful. He was still young enough to yearn to live in freedom instead of scraping by under the thumb of a communist bureaucrat. At some point, they might be rounded up and die in a re-education camp like Cara. His surviving son had been sent to a camp after surrendering. Two years later, he was still there but too far north for them to visit.

Uncle Bao visited a wealthy friend in Can Tho, who was also of Hòa lineage and whose businesses were being seized by the communists. Mr. Văn Quang had the foresight to transfer much of his wealth to a Swiss bank when it was apparent that the South was going to lose the war. Still, like many, he hoped there would be some national reconciliation, but when his businesses were seized, he knew it was not in the cards.

The Boat People

Together, Quang and Bao pooled their available savings and began looking for a boat. The communists were scrutinizing boat sales, so they developed a plan to buy a 35-foot river freighter they could use to transport goods while they plotted their escape. Quang would use his remaining aggregate business to cover the boat's real purpose, escaping Vietnam. It was just a matter of time before his aggregate business would be taken to construct government infrastructure, so he had to act fast.

Quang's son, Văn, had to learn to be a river pilot and develop the navigational skills necessary to cross the open ocean. The plan to escape by boat would take longer than they had hoped. Keeping it a secret within a tight-knit family group was the only way to avoid detection by the police and authorities.

Quang secured a contract to tow a gravel barge from Can Tho for a road-building project in Cau Ma. Văn operated the boat and would haul bags of cooking charcoal back upstream to Can Tho. As the plan developed, Văn learned the etiquette required to bribe checkpoint police and government officials for extra allotments of fuel and drinking water, which he would hoard for the long ocean journey. There were six checkpoints between Can Tho and the ocean. He would have to figure out when they were unmanned so they could escape downriver undetected. Văn built a false bottom in the boat to store the fuel, rice, and water and to make a place for the refugees to hide on the downriver run. It would be cramped.

Many former officials in the Viet Cong's Provisional Revolutionary Government were disenchanted and bitter about their exclusion when the North took control of the South's government. They had expected to be included as partners in the new government, but instead, they were shunted aside, given low-level clerical jobs and a small plot of land to grow vegetables.

The Northerners considered the Viet Cong to be untrustworthy. Not one member of the PRG held a position of authority in the new communist regime.

Many PRG members had relatives in the South's military and government before it fell. They watched as their kin were shuttled off to internment and hard labor in the re-education camps. They were initially told to pack for a two-week stay when, in fact, they were imprisoned at hard labor for years. Many Viet Cong and PRG members had become pariahs to their own families as the North's oppression unfolded.

Quang was shocked when Anh Trí, a former Deputy Minister of Justice in the PRG, approached him about buying their new boat. He was suspicious of Trí's intent and thought his inquiry might be a setup. Quang knew the Anh family in Can Tho. One of Trí's brothers was an ARVN Army officer, and another was an administrator in one of President Thieu's government offices in Saigon. Trí had joined the Viet Cong and disappeared around 1965. He had only seen his parents a few times in all those years.

Quang told Trí the boat was not for sale. He wondered if Trí had somehow learned of their plans. Trí said he wanted to develop the boat into a fishing boat, which Quang knew was a lie. His freighter would have to be completely re-rigged at great expense for fishing. The hull was not designed or suitable for ocean fishing. But he did not say anything to deter Trí. He asked him to bring a list of the investors participating in his purchase. He wanted the list in part to smoke out Trí's intent.

Quang knew Trí's parents. The Anhs were disillusioned with their son's involvement with the Viet Cong. He invited Trí's father, Huan, to lunch to see if he could learn more about his son's intent. The family had been estranged from their son for years until recently, when he came over to apologize for his absence and express dissatisfaction with the North's failure to reconcile with those who had opposed them in the South.

During the reunion with his parents, Trí attempted to assure them that he had nothing to do with the detention of his brothers. One brother, who served as an ARVN officer, had been executed. His other brother was sent to a re-education camp. Trí himself had been shunted aside in the new communist government after years of sacrifice for the revolution. His father could tell he was bitter.

In recounting Trí's visit, Huan told Quang that Trí's mother yelled at him to get out. "Maybe I will forgive you one day, but not today. Get out!" she said.

Trí returned to Quang's house a week later with a list of investors. He was unaware that Quang had visited his parents. It was apparent to Quang these were not investors but family members and their children, who were trying to escape the country. Trí's wife, her sisters, and his parents were on the list. Quang was stunned.

"This is a curious list," Quang said, looking into Trí's eyes for signs of deception. "I know your parents; they are not fishermen."

"Yes, I know. I hope they will join me on this journey," Trí replied. "It is the only way to redeem myself with my family for what has happened."

"Contact me in a month, and I will give you a price," Quang said. Now, it was clear to both men what they were discussing without saying it.

Quang visited Trí's father, Huan, and confirmed that he had discussed leaving the country with Trí. Huan and his wife wanted to escape with their two daughters and their children but had no viable plan. Quang told him about their boat and that they planned to leave after the monsoon season in 1978. The price would be $3,000 for adults and $1,500 per child, payable in gold.

It would be another few months before the boat was ready. Văn spent the time observing river checkpoints and developing relationships with the river police. He discovered the checkpoints were not always manned late in the day on weekends when river traffic slowed, and the police took time off to drink. He also studied the tide charts. Once at the mouth of the Mekong, he would have to run to international waters at high tide to avoid getting stuck on the sandbars. He needed to be clear of the coast before daylight when the fishing boats and police patrols emerged into the coastal waters.

The day arrived in the summer of 1978 for the escape. Uncle Bao and Aunt Hòa boarded a bus to Long Xuyen with Linh. Long Xuyen was 20 miles upstream from Can Tho and 80 miles from the mouth of the Mekong. The authorities did not expect refugees to depart that far upriver, so there would be less scrutiny at the dock, especially on the weekend. A total of 16 people had committed to escape Vietnam on the boat, including six young children. Văn and a crew member would complete the list of 18 persons.

Văn had arranged for his passengers to arrive in small groups at staggered times from the back of a restaurant near the docks on the evening before the launch.

Then, every half hour in darkness, he escorted a small group to the boat to avoid attracting the police's attention. They would go below deck into the hold to wait until all the subscribers had arrived with one bag of clothes and their valuables.

Uncle Bao stored his stash of jewelry and gold, along with Cara's lock box, in a waterproof metal compartment in the bilges below the false deck. Bags of rice, cans of fuel, and water were also stored in the secret hold. All 16 passengers would hide there for the 20-hour trip downriver into the sea, taking a few breaks for fresh air when Văn signaled that it was safe to come topside.

At dawn, with the nervous refugees settled in the stuffy, cramped hideaway, Văn started the engine, ferried out into the Mekong's monsoon-swollen current, and headed for the coast. Only two checkpoints were manned that weekend. Văn motored up to the patrol boat docked at the checkpoint instead of waiting for them to chase him down for an inspection. The officer jumped on board, and Văn slipped him a bribe. Only one of the checkpoint officers bothered to lift the hatch briefly and look in the hold below deck before waving Văn on. The passengers sat quietly in the hold below the false deck. Văn's foresight in developing relationships with the police had paid off. They did not suspect him.

The boat made it to the mouth of the Mekong at about 2:00 AM. The refugees slowly emerged from their stuffy quarters as the boat rode over the swells and headed out to sea. Văn had killed the running lights after passing the last checkpoint. The boat was a ghostly vessel running low when it suddenly came to a halt. The engine revved. The propeller was tangled in a fishing net between two poles in the shallow seabed off the coast. Văn had not seen the poles in the dark. He would have to jump into the water over the transom to cut away the net but could not do that until first light. After dawn, they would be at risk of being seen by the fishermen and coastal patrol boats. Police were on most of the seaworthy fishing boats to prevent them from joining the exodus from Vietnam by "the boat people."

As the first hint of pink light illuminated the eastern sky, Văn slipped into the water with his knife. Twenty minutes later, he cleared the last of the net from the propeller and was ready to get underway. A few fishing boats could be seen emerging from the mouth of the river. He revved the engine and headed for international waters at full speed into the open ocean.

At Sea

As the freighter entered international waters, the passengers were joyous even though a perilous journey lay ahead. Văn seemed to have thought of everything. He had one set of binoculars he gave to his father to look southward for Poulo Condore, the infamous island prison now under the control of the communist regime. He wanted to avoid getting close to the island where lookouts might see the boat and send a patrol boat to capture them. If captured, they would never leave Poulo Condore alive.

Văn wanted to get as far into international waters as possible before heading southwest toward Malaysia and the sea lanes leading to their rescue. After two hours at sea, Văn turned the freighter to the south-southwest. Quang saw a feint outline of an island, which he believed was Poulo Condore, so Văn changed bearing to due west until the island was astern and fell below the horizon.

Two hours after passing Poulo Condore, a trawler appeared on the horizon, closing fast. Văn feared that the communist regime had seen them from Poulo Condore and called a patrol boat. Văn had a pistol but could not win a shoot-out with the Vietnam Navy vessel. The trawler pulled alongside, but the sailors had no uniforms or weapons other than machetes and knives. They jumped from the higher trawler deck onto Văn's boat.

Quang shouted, "Thai fishermen," which relieved the refugees of fears of being killed by the barbaric professional pirates who preyed on the boat people leaving Vietnam. The fishermen searched the bags below decks and took jewelry, Văn's compass, and binoculars. They left the bags of rice in the hold and never found the secret compartment below the false deck. Uncle Bao's stash of valuables was safe.

Before departing, one of the Thais pointed to the south and, in Vietnamese, said, "ships."

Văn turned the boat to the south, noticing the location of the sun, which would be his only navigation aid now that the compass was gone. The boat motored south for five more days as the refugees grew increasingly hungry, tired and dirty. They entered shipping lanes, but the freighters and tankers that hoped would rescue them just sailed by. A few deckhands waved but offered no assistance. High clouds were now on the horizon in the east at sunset, which meant a front was moving in. They had enjoyed gentle seas up until this point, but Văn's vessel did not have a bow rise to repulse heavy seas. It was a riverboat, not designed for crossing oceans.

Eight days after leaving the mouth of the Mekong, Văn was napping when his helmsman noticed a faint light on the horizon. The crewman awakened Văn. In another hour, they could see the lights of what appeared to be an oil rig. Văn reduced his speed to avoid approaching the rig in the dark.

At dawn, with the rig less than 500 yards away, Văn began his approach. Crew members were already at the railing when he pulled alongside. Văn said in English, "Rescue, please."

The rig manager was on a radio phone. He looked down on the motley refugees and said in English, with a British accent. "No, we cannot rescue you. Indonesia says they have too many boat people."

Văn told the passengers to get life jackets and their bags while he asked the rig boss, "Just let us come aboard to rest for a while to rest and eat."

The rig manager told Văn to wait while he spoke with headquarters.

There were only six life jackets for 18 people. Having more on board would have aroused suspicions among the police when they inspected the boat. The adult women were told to wear them and hold the children. Văn instructed his crew member to give the empty water and fuel cans to use as flotation.

Then Văn said, "Drop your clothes bags and get into the water!"

They looked at him incredulously. Uncle Bao had retrieved his bag of valuables. He could not swim and did not want to leave the boat holding onto an empty fuel can.

"Hold the children. Jump into the water. They will be forced to rescue us," Văn exclaimed.

Aunt Hòa told Uncle Bao to follow her and hold on to her jacket. She jumped into the water, holding Linh, who broke away as they hit the water. The seven-year-old flailed at the water, reaching for her aunt. Another woman in a life jacket grabbed her by the hair and pulled her to the surface into Hòa's arms.

Văn emptied the last can of diesel fuel in the hold, set the rudder and throttle to move the boat out to sea, and threw a match in the hold as he jumped off the transom. Meanwhile, the rig manager was screaming into a radio phone, gesturing wildly to his bosses in a faraway office. The flaming boat drifted away as the American and British rig crew gathered up the refugees. Trí thought how ironic it was that Americans, whom he had fought for years as a member of the PRG, were saving his life.

As soon as the rig crew saw the refugees entering the water, they threw life rings and deployed a rescue raft. Others slid down the ladders at high speed and entered the water to help those struggling to stay afloat. One of the crew members reached Uncle Hòa just before he went under. He was still gripping his box of valuables.

After a couple of days on the rig, a boat from Indonesia, paid for by the oil company, arrived to pick up the refugees and take them to a camp on Galang Island. The rig workers also took up a collection to give to the women with children.

By 1978, the trickle of refugees leaving Vietnam by boat had grown to a torrent, especially among the Hòa. Thousands died at sea, victims of storms and pirates. In June 1979, 350,000 Vietnamese populated refugee camps in Southeast Asia and Hong Kong.[32] The exodus would continue into the early 1990s.

For the Nguyens and Linh, a new life was beginning. The most perilous leg of their journey to freedom was over.

---

[32] https://en.wikipedia.org/wiki/Vietnamese_boat_people.

The Orphan

"Dad, you got an envelope from someone in France," Melissa Harding yelled to her dad from the back door. Josh was hooking up the horse trailer to take his twelve-year-old daughter to a riding lesson up the road in Johnson City. Melissa's mother, Betsy, was away at a nursing conference, so Josh was enjoying a special weekend with his daughter.

"Okay, put it in the cab. I will look at it later," Harding replied.

Upon arriving at Holston Glen Stables, Josh and Melissa saddled up her horse, Sydney, and she began her hunter jumper lesson. Josh glanced at the envelope from a Paris address, slipped it between the seat and console, and turned his attention to his daughter's riding lesson.

On the way home, Melissa asked, "Who is the letter from?"

"I don't really know. Probably someone wanting to know about work stuff," Harding replied. "I haven't opened it."

He was now the executive director of the State Agricultural Association and often got inquiries from all over the world about various issues but had never received inquiries from France.

After getting home and unloading, Melissa went to her room to do homework. Josh retrieved the envelope and went upstairs to his study to open it. He pulled out the handwritten letter. Three snapshots were taped to a flat of cardboard.

One was a picture of a scrap of paper of his handwriting with his name and address at Stabron20, FPO, San Francisco, CA.

"Holy cow!" is all he could think as he hurriedly turned to the letter.

Dear Mr. Harding,

My name is Nguyen Hoa Linh. I am 21 years old and was born in Saigon in 1971. I left Vietnam on a boat in 1978 with my aunt and uncle. We were known by many as "the boat people" who fled Vietnam after the communist takeover in 1975. My mother, Nguyen Cara, died in a communist camp in Vietnam in 1975.

Last year, before she died, my aunt gave me my mother's lockbox and asked me to open it. She showed me this scrap of paper with your name on it. My mother told my aunt that this was the name of my father, whom she had met when she worked at a club in Saigon in 1970. I have also included my photograph and an old picture of my mother, which is somewhat faded.

Recently, the U.S. Citizenship and Immigration Service granted my application to become a permanent resident of the United States. The U.S. Embassy here in Paris helped me with the application based on the evidence presented to them, which is how I found your address in Tennessee. While I do have contacts in the Vietnamese community in the United States, my strongest desire is to find my father.

I will be flying into Atlanta next month and want to meet you if that is possible. I will stay temporarily with a Vietnamese family connected to a relief organization for Amerasians. Because my schedule is uncertain, I will call you after I arrive in Atlanta in hopes that you will take time to meet with me.

I know this letter will probably shock you. Rest assured that I do not want to cause problems for you or your family. I am just seeking my father, who, if I can find him, is the only family I have left.

Sincerely,

Linh

Josh Harding looked at Linh's photo, which a professional had taken. The margin had the U.S. Embassy, Paris, printed on it. He immediately recognized a hint of his features on the pretty girl's face. There was also a copy of a letter from the U.S. Citizenship and Immigration Services granting her admission and residence in the U.S. under the Amerasian Act, which was passed to facilitate immigration by Amerasian orphans.

The Meeting

When Betsy returned from her trip, Josh told her he needed to talk with her in private about something that he did not want Melissa to overhear.

"What this about?" Besty asked.

"I got a letter from a young woman in Paris who says she thinks she is my daughter from a relationship I had with a Vietnamese woman I met in a club in Saigon in 1970," Josh said, handing her the envelope. "Look it over, and let's meet for lunch tomorrow. I know it will be hard, but let's wait to talk more then. I am going to have a hard time sleeping tonight, so I am going to sleep on the couch."

They met her for lunch at a Mexican restaurant in Knoxville while Melissa was at school. "Okay, I get the picture. I presume this woman was a prostitute whom you had sex with during a one-night stand?" Besty said.

"It was actually two nights, but yes, you have the picture. Honestly, at the time, I did not know whether I was going to survive for another month, so I was looking for any comfort available," Josh said. "She was very nice, and I was attracted to her and her story. These women were not like the trashy hookers on the streets here. It was different but hard to explain."

"Do you think the girl from Paris is honest, or is there something else going on?" Besty said.

"She has the note I gave to her mother. It's my handwriting. Look at her face. I think there is a good possibility she is my daughter. She should be 21 now," Josh responded.

"Okay, let's meet her in Atlanta. Let me handle Melissa," Betsy said with a voice that conveyed understanding. "I will tell her we will meet someone from your dad's military service days. Melissa can stay with one of our friends while we go on the trip. If we meet with this woman and she seems honest, I will talk to Melissa about it when we return."

Betsy's meeting with Melissa did not go as planned. Melissa was smart and asked what was going on. "Is this related to that letter he got from a woman in Paris?"

At that point, Betsy told Melissa to sit down. They were planning to meet an orphan who thought she might be her dad's daughter from Vietnam. "We are going to meet her and sort it out," Betsy said.

"Can I come with you?" Melissa asked.

"No, let us see if this is legitimate. The young woman is just seeking her father, and she doesn't know for sure, so we will do some testing. But let's keep this in the family for now," Besty said. "The Vietnamese woman is an adult now and is resettling in the United States to look for her father after her aunt in Paris died."

After Linh's arrival in the U.S., she called Josh's office number, and they arranged a meeting. Josh and Betsy had already decided how to handle the meeting. If it appeared that Linh was Josh's daughter, they would invite her to visit and stay in the garage apartment at the farm while the DNA testing results came back.

Betsy told Josh that she was inclined to see if she could help Linh, whether she was his daughter. But that would depend in part on the meeting and what Linh wanted. Having lost her mother at a young age, Betsy understood the trauma she must have gone through as an unwanted orphan.

Linh was waiting for them inside the door of the Vietnam House Restaurant in Sandy Springs. Like her mother, Linh was trim and pretty. Betsy hugged her to put her at ease, and they found a booth in the back of the restaurant.

Linh thanked Josh and Besty for driving down to meet with her. She opened the envelope and pulled out the original note with Josh's name and address. Josh looked at her face and saw his features. He knew immediately that she was his daughter but could not admit to it until DNA testing confirmed their relationship. He had a lump in his throat and could no longer talk. Linh was calm and poised. Betsy took over the conversation. Josh asked to be excused and went to the bathroom to gather himself.

Betsy told Linh they wanted her to visit them in Holston City and that she would arrange for DNA testing at the hospital where she worked. The test would require a blood draw. Linh agreed and said she wanted that, too, but she had a job interview with Delta Airlines and could not come for a few days. The airlines were looking for multilingual stewardesses, and she was optimistic she could get a job. Her degree was in Finance, but this job would help her get her feet on the ground while staying in contact with her Vietnamese friends in Paris.

Betsy told her to call when she knew her availability, and they would buy her an airline ticket and meet her at the Knoxville airport.

On the drive home, Josh and Betsy discussed their plan. The challenge now was how to present the situation to Melissa. Betsy knew she would have to be the one to help Melissa with any lingering anxiety. They also wondered if Linh would be happy in Tennessee, which would be a culture shock given her upbringing in Paris.

During the trip to meet Linh, Melissa stayed with a retired nurse who had helped Betsy when she first went to work at the hospital. Janice Newton did not have children, so she became Melissa's godmother. She had been a regular babysitter since Melissa was a toddler. Betsy had told Janice about Linh and that it was best not to say much until they sorted things out.

Janice dropped Melissa off at the farm and picked up a dozen fresh eggs Betsy set aside for her. She hugged Melissa goodbye. Josh and Betsy took Melissa to the living room to discuss their visit with Linh.

"Well, what's the story?" Melissa asked.

"There is a good possibility she is my daughter and your sister," Josh responded.

"Oh great! Is she going to move in too?" Melissa asked.

"We are going to invite her to visit and get DNA testing done to determine if your father is her dad," Betsy responded. "She is looking for work in Atlanta now."

"If she is my daughter, I will still love you just as much as ever. I will need to help her as my daughter," Josh said. "She has been an orphan living with her aunt in Paris since they fled Vietnam in 1978."

Then Melissa said emphatically, "You slept with a prostitute, didn't you, Dad? What are the people in church going to say about that?"

"How many people at church are perfect? Zero. How many of them want to be forgiven for their transgressions when they were young? All of them!" Josh said. Betsy took Melissa to the back porch to sit in the swing and discuss things.

Seven days later, Josh met Linh at the airport in Knoxville and drove her back to Holston City. Upon arriving at the farm, Josh showed her the garage apartment and took her to the barn to see the horses. Dinner was planned that evening at home with Betsy and Melissa. Melissa was quiet throughout the dinner. Betsy asked Linh about Paris, and much of the conversation revolved around her upbringing there.

The next day, Josh drove Linh to the hospital to draw blood. The test would take at least a week before the results would come back. Betsy asked them to run two batches so there could be no doubt about the results. They visited the Vietnamese restaurant in West Knoxville. The owner was delighted to meet Linh and offered her a job on the spot, but it was a long drive from Holston City, and Linh didn't drive.

When DNA results came back a week later, Betsy called from work to let Josh know the results. When Betsy got home from work, they planned a meeting with Linh, who had started helping cook dinner every night while Melissa did her homework. She prepared delicious French and Vietnamese dishes and seemed to fit in comfortably without intruding, spending her days reading and writing. Linh was slicing carrots when they walked into the kitchen. Melissa was upstairs in her room.

"We have the results," Josh said. "Welcome home!"

He gave her a big hug with tears in his eyes. Linh wiped away her own tears.

"Thank you so much," Linh said, crying with relief and joy. Betsy left them alone and went upstairs to talk with Melissa, who had already resigned herself to the fact that she had a sister. Melissa had this uncanny ability at her age to look for solutions, not problems and told her mom everything would be alright.

Settling Down

While Linh's search for her father ended, her adult life was just beginning. She turned down a job offer from Delta and started to look for work in Knoxville to be close to her new family. Betsy helped her get an appointment with the dean of the Language Department at the University, after which she was offered a job as a special assistant to the dean, assisting French-speaking students in the University program.

After working at the University for a few months, Linh was accepted into the MBA program at the College of Business. She earned her master's degree two years later. She was hired almost immediately as a financial analyst by an international engineering firm working out of Oak Ridge, specializing in managing their overseas projects. Linh visited Harding's farm on the weekends and attended Melissa's equestrian competitions. Linh would eventually marry an engineer from her firm, settle in West Knoxville with her husband, and give birth to two children.

An estimated 100,000 orphans were fathered by the more than 3 million Americans who served in Vietnam from 1965 to 1974.[33] Only about 3% found their biological fathers. Eventually, about 26,000 orphans and 75,000 of their Vietnamese family members were resettled in the United States.[34]

Linh knew she was more fortunate than most Vietnam War orphans. So, she volunteered to assist a nonprofit helping orphans of the Vietnam War find their fathers and get resettled in the U.S. For her, the long journey from Saigon was finally complete.

The End.

---

[33] Nguyen Phan Que Mai, She searched for a father she'd never met. Then, after 52 years, they found each other. USA Today, March 14, 2023.

[34] David Lamb, Children of the Vietnam War, Smithsonian Magazine, June 2009.

Vietnam War Timeline from Wikipedia

Early 20th-century (1913–1949)

1919–The Council of Four ignores a petition written by Ho Chí Minh seeking Vietnamese independence from French rule.[10]

1941–Franklin D. Roosevelt declines repeated requests from the French to assist France's attempts to recolonize Vietnam.[11]

July 1945–Members of the Office of Strategic Services (OSS), commanded by Major Allison Thomas, parachute into Vietnam to help train Viet Minh forces for operations against occupying Japanese forces.[12]

August 15, 1945–Japan surrenders to the Allies of World War II. In Indochina, the Japanese administration allows Hồ Chí Minh to take control of the country in the August Revolution. Hồ Chí Minh fights with a variety of other political factions for control of the major cities.

August 1945–A few days after the August Revolution, Nationalist Chinese forces entered from the north and, as previously planned by the Allies, established an administration in the country as far south as the 16th parallel north.

September 26, 1945: OSS officer Lieutenant Colonel A. Peter Dewey — who was working with the Viet Minh to repatriate Americans captured by the Japanese– was killed by a member of the Viet Minh who mistakenly believed him to be French.

October 1945–British troops landed in southern Vietnam and established a provisional administration. The British freed French soldiers and officials imprisoned by the Japanese. The French begin taking control of cities within the British zone of occupation.

February 1946—The French signed an agreement with China. France gives up its concessions in Shanghai and other Chinese ports. In exchange, China agrees to assist the French in returning to Vietnam north of the 17th parallel.

March 6, 1946—After negotiations with the Chinese and the Viet Minh, the French signed an agreement recognizing Vietnam within the French Union. Shortly after, the French landed at Haiphong and occupied the rest of northern Vietnam. The Viet Minh used the negotiating process with France and China to buy time to use their armed forces to destroy all competing nationalist groups in the north.

December 1946—Negotiations between the Viet Minh and the French broke down. The Viet Minh are driven out of Hanoi into the countryside.

1947-1949—The Viet Minh fought a limited insurgency in remote rural areas of northern Vietnam.

1949—Chinese communists reach the northern border of Indochina. The Viet Minh drove the French from the border region and began to receive large amounts of weapons from the Soviet Union and China. The weapons transform the Viet Minh from an irregular, large-scale insurgent movement into a conventional army.

1950s

May 1, 1950—After the capture of Hainan Island from Chinese Nationalist forces by the Chinese People's Liberation Army, President Truman approves $10 million in military assistance for anti-communist efforts in Indochina. The Defense Attaché Office was established in Saigon in May 1950, a formal recognition of Vietnam (vice French Indochina). This was the beginning of formal U.S. military personnel assignments in Vietnam. U.S. Naval, Army and Air Force personnel established their respective attachés at this time.

September 1950—Truman sends the Military Assistance Advisory Group (MAAG) Indochina to Vietnam to assist the French. The President claimed they were not sent as combat troops but to supervise the use of $10 million worth of U.S. military equipment to support the French in their effort to fight the Viet Minh forces.

Following the outbreak of the Korean War, Truman announced "acceleration in the furnishing of military assistance to the forces of France and the Associated

States in Indochina…." and sent 123 non-combat troops to help with supplies to fight against the communist Viet Minh.

1951–Truman authorizes $150 million in French support.

1953–By November, the French commander in Indochina, General Navarre, asked U.S. General McArthur to loan 12 Fairchild C-119 aircraft to be flown by French crews to facilitate Operation Castor at Dien Bien Phú.

1954–In January, Navarre's Deputy asked for additional transport aircraft. Negotiations ended on March 3 with 24 CIA pilots (CAT) to operate 12 U.S. Air Force C-119s, flying undercover using French insignia but maintained by the USAF.[13]

1954–General Paul Ely, the French Chief of Staff, proposed an American operation to rescue French forces. Operation Vulture was hastily planned but not approved because of a lack of consensus.[14][15]

May 6, 1954–James B. McGovern Jr. and Wallace Buford, U.S. civilian contract pilots employed by Civil Air Transport and flying a C-119 inscribed with French Air Force insignia, were killed when their aircraft was hit by ground fire and crashed after making a parachute drop to resupply French troops at Dien Bien Phú.[16][17]

1954–The Viet Minh defeat the French at the Battle of Dien Bien Phú. The defeat, along with the end of the Korean War the previous year, causes the French to seek a negotiated settlement to the war.

1954–The Geneva Conference, called to determine the post-French future of Indochina, proposes a temporary division of Vietnam, to be followed by nationwide elections to unify the country in 1956. However, the final declaration was left unsigned by all delegates after the United States and the State of Vietnam stated they wouldn't accept the proposal.[18]

1954–Two months after the Geneva conference, North Vietnam formed Group 100 with headquarters at Ban Namèo. Its purpose was to direct, organize, train and supply the Pathet Lao to gain control of Laos, which, along with Cambodia and Vietnam, formed French Indochina.

1955–North Vietnam launches an 'anti-landlord' campaign, during which counter-revolutionaries are imprisoned or killed. The numbers killed or imprisoned are disputed, with historian Stanley Karnow estimating about 6,000 while others (see the book "Fire in the Lake") estimate only 800. Rudolph Rummel puts the figure as high as 200,000.[19]

November 1, 1955–President Eisenhower deploys the MAAG to train the Army of the Republic of Vietnam. This marks the official beginning of American involvement in the war, as recognized by the Vietnam Veterans Memorial.[20]

April 1956–The last French troops finally withdraw from Vietnam.

1954-1956–450,000 Vietnamese civilians fled the Viet Minh administration in North Vietnam and relocated to South Vietnam as part of the U.S. government's Operation Passage to Freedom. Approximately 52,000 move in the opposite direction.

1956–National unification elections do not occur.

December 1958–North Vietnam invades Laos and occupies parts of the country.

July 8, 1959–Chester M. Ovnand and Dale R. Buis become the first two American Advisors to die in Vietnam.[21]

September 1959–North Vietnam forms Group 959, which assumes command of the Pathet Lao forces in Laos.

1960s

November 1960–A coup attempt by paratroopers was foiled after Diệm falsely promised reform, allowing loyalists to crush the rebels.

December 20, 1960–The National Liberation Front of South Vietnam (NLF) is founded.

January 1961–Soviet Premier Nikita Khrushchev pledges support for "wars of national liberation" throughout the world. The idea of creating a neutral Laos is suggested to Kennedy.

May 1961–Kennedy sent 400 United States Army Special Forces personnel to South Vietnam to train South Vietnamese soldiers following a visit to the country by Vice President Johnson.[22]

June 1961–Kennedy meets with Khrushchev in Vienna. He protested North Vietnam's attacks on Laos and pointed out that the U.S. was supporting the neutrality of Laos. The two leaders agree to pursue a policy of creating a neutral Laos.

June 1961–Kennedy said, "Now we have a problem making our power credible and Vietnam looks like the place" to James Reston of The New York Times (immediately after meeting Khrushchev in Vienna).

August 10, 1961–A test run of the U.S. herbicidal warfare program in South Vietnam. ("Operation Trail Dust")

October 1961–Following successful NLF attacks, Defense Secretary Robert S. McNamara recommends sending six divisions (200,000 men) to Vietnam.

February 8, 1962–The Military Assistance Command Vietnam (MACV) is created by President Kennedy.

February 1962–The attempted assassination of Diệm by two dissident Republic of Vietnam Air Force pilots who bombed his palace fails.

July 23, 1962–The International Agreement on the Neutrality of Laos was signed in Geneva, promising Laotian neutrality.

August 1, 1962–Kennedy signed the Foreign Assistance Act of 1962, which provides "… military assistance to countries which are on the rim of the Communist world and under direct attack."

October 1962–Operation Ranch Hand begins. U.S. planes spray herbicides and defoliants over South Vietnam until 1971.

January 3, 1963–NLF victory in the Battle of Ap Bac.

May 8, 1963–Buddhists demonstrate in Huế, South Vietnam, after the display of religious flags was prohibited during the celebration of Vesak, Gautama Buddha's birthday; but Catholic flags celebrating the consecration of Archbishop Ngô Đình Thục, brother of Ngô Đình Diệm, were not prohibited. The police of Ngô Đình Cẩn, Diệm's younger brother, open fire, killing nine.

May 1963–Republican Barry Goldwater declares that the U.S. should fight to win or withdraw from Vietnam. Later on, during his presidential campaign against Lyndon B. Johnson, his Democratic opponents accuse him of wanting to use nuclear weapons in the conflict.

June 11, 1963–Photographs of protesting Buddhist monk Thích Quảng Đức, burning himself to death in protest in Saigon, appear in U.S. newspapers.

Summer 1963–Madame Nhu, de facto First Lady to the bachelor Diệm, makes a series of vitriolic attacks on Buddhists, calling the immolations "barbecues." Diệm ignores U.S. calls to silence her.

August 21, 1963–ARVN special forces loyal to Ngô Đình Nhu, younger brother of Diệm, stage raids across the country, attacking Buddhist temples and firing on monks. The cremated remains of Thích Quảng Đức are confiscated from Xá Lợi Pagoda in Saigon. New U.S. ambassador Henry Cabot Lodge rebukes Diệm by visiting Xá Lợi and giving refuge to Buddhist leader Thích Trí Quang. The U.S. calls for Nhu to be dropped by Diệm and threatens to cut aid to Colonel Lê Quang Tung's Special Forces if they are not sent into battle rather than used to repress dissidents.

September 2, 1963–Kennedy criticizes the Diệm regime in an interview with Walter Cronkite, citing the Buddhist repression and claiming that Diệm was out of touch.

Late October 1963–Nhu, unaware that Saigon region commander General Tôn Thất Đình is double-crossing him, draws up plans for a phony coup and counter-coup to reaffirm the Diệm regime. Đình sends Nhu's loyal special forces out of Saigon on the pretext of fighting communists and in readiness for the counter-coup and rings Saigon with rebel troops.

November 1, 1963–Military officers launch a coup d'état against Diệm, with the tacit approval of the Kennedy administration. Diệm and Nhu escape the presidential residence via a secret exit after loyalist forces were locked out of Saigon, unable to rescue them.

November 2, 1963–Diệm and Nhu are discovered in nearby Cholon. Although they had been promised exile by the junta, they were executed by Nguyễn Văn Nhung, the bodyguard of General Dương Văn Minh. Minh leads the military junta.

November 1963–By this time, Kennedy had increased the number of military personnel from the 900 that were there when he became president to 16,000 just before his death.[23]

November 22, 1963–Kennedy is assassinated in Dallas, Texas.

August 1964–Gulf of Tonkin incident: *USS Maddox* is allegedly attacked by North Vietnamese patrol torpedo boats in the Gulf of Tonkin (the attack is later disputed), leading President Johnson to call for air strikes on North Vietnamese patrol boat bases. Two U.S. aircraft are shot down, and one U.S. pilot, Everett Alvarez, Jr., becomes the first U.S. airman to be taken prisoner by North Vietnam. Congress passes the Gulf of Tonkin Resolution, authorizing U.S. military action to support any Southeast Asia Treaty Organization government against communist aggression.

March 2, 1965–Operation Rolling Thunder begins.

March 8, 1965–First U.S. ground troops arrive in Da Nang composed of 3,500 U.S. Marines of the 3rd Marine Division on Okinawa.[24][25]

March 10, 1965–Authored in secret with roots in at least 1964, "Plan of Action for South Vietnam" was a top-secret rolling document and evolving plan that outlined a significant departure from the public narrative: eradicating communism in Indochina to "avoiding a humiliating U.S. defeat." The report is infamously dated both 10 and 24 March 1965—months and ultimately years before the bulk of U.S. ground troops were to be deployed.[26]

July 28, 1965–In a nationally televised speech, President Johnson announced his decision to send an additional 50,000 American troops to South Vietnam, increasing the number of personnel there by two-thirds and bringing the commitment to 125,000. Johnson also said that the monthly draft call would more than double to more than 1,000 new young men per day (from 17,000 to 35,000) for enlistment and training in the U.S. Armed Forces.

1966–Lyndon B. Johnson expanded the number of troops being sent into Vietnam to 385,000.

October 1966–Secretary of Defense Robert S. McNamara initiates Project 100,000, significantly reducing recruitment standards for the U.S. military in the face of rising manpower needs.[27][28]

April 20, 1969–Nixon orders the withdrawal of 150,000 U.S. troops from South Vietnam over the span of 12 months, citing Vietnamization; U.S. troop presence peaks at over 540,000.[1]

June 8, 1969–Nixon announces that 25,000 U.S. troops would be withdrawn by the end of September. A month later, troops would begin departing South Vietnam.

July 25, 1969–The Nixon Doctrine was announced at an informal press conference by President Nixon.

July 30, 1969–President Nixon visits South Vietnam for the first and only time.

October 15, 1969–Hundreds of thousands of people attend mass protests across the United States for the United States to withdraw from the Vietnam War.

November 15, 1969–A second, larger protest takes place in Washington, D.C., with an estimated 500,000 people.

December 1, 1969–The first draft lottery since 1942 is held.

1970s

April 20, 1970–Nixon announces a second withdrawal of 150,000 U.S. troops from South Vietnam over the span of 12 months.

April 30, 1970–Nixon announces that U.S. troops were sent into Cambodia, reversing his April 20 decision to withdraw 150,000 troops.[29]

June 3, 1970–Nixon withdraws half of the 31,000 troops in Cambodia to fight in South Vietnam.

January 6, 1971–Secretary of Defense Melvin Laird says that the combat mission of U.S. troops was planned to end by summer.

March 1, 1971–At 1:32 a.m., a bomb planted by Weather Underground explodes outside the U.S. Capitol in protest of the invasion of Laos.

April 23, 1971 - A protest tantamount to the November 1969 protest takes place in Washington, D.C.

June 13, 1971–The Pentagon Papers begin to be published.

July 26, 1971–Kissinger announces plans for $7.5 billion in aid to be provided for Vietnam and for the removal of all U.S. troops within nine months.

January 13, 1972–Nixon announces plans for 70,000 U.S. troops to be pulled out of Vietnam, half of the remaining forces.

February 21, 1972–Nixon met Mao Zedong and became the first president in U.S. history to meet with a Chinese Communist leader face to face.

April 20, 1972–Nixon announces plans to reduce U.S. troops in South Vietnam to 49,000 by July 1, 1972.

August 29, 1972–Nixon announced the further withdrawal of U.S. troops from South Vietnam to only 27,000 by December 1, 1972.

November 7, 1972–Nixon wins re-election.

January 22, 1973–Lyndon B. Johnson dies.

January 27, 1973–U.S. troops are planned to be withdrawn from South Vietnam in 60 days because of the signing of the Paris Peace Accords. North Vietnam and Nixon also agree to withdraw troops from Cambodia and Laos.

March 29, 1973–The last American combat troops are withdrawn from Vietnam.

August 9, 1974–Richard Nixon resigned because of the Watergate scandal and was succeeded by Gerald Ford.

December 1974. North Vietnam ignores the Paris Peace Accords and invades the South.

April 17, 1975–The Khmer Rouge took Phnom Penh, ending the Cambodian Civil War.

April 30, 1975–General Minh surrenders to North Vietnam, ending the war.

December 23, 1978–The Cambodian Khmer Rouge opened fire on the Socialist Republic of Vietnam's border provinces.

December 25, 1978–The Socialist Republic of Vietnam responds by invading Cambodia with 150,000 soldiers, taking control of the country in two weeks.

January 8, 1979–A pro-Vietnam government is established in Phnom Penh, and the ten-year occupation of Cambodia by the Socialist Republic of Vietnam begins.

March 1992–A UN peacekeeping force, the United Nations Transitional Authority in Cambodia, began monitoring Cambodia.

May 1993–Free elections were held but were boycotted by the Khmer Rouge.

September 24, 1993–A new constitution was ratified, under which the Cambodian monarchy was restored. Norodom Sihanouk returned to the throne.

1997–The Extraordinary Chambers in the Courts of Cambodia, a tribunal for the Khmer Rouge, was established.

April 15, 1998–Death of Pol Pot.

U.S. Coast Guard Map of Mekong Delta 1970

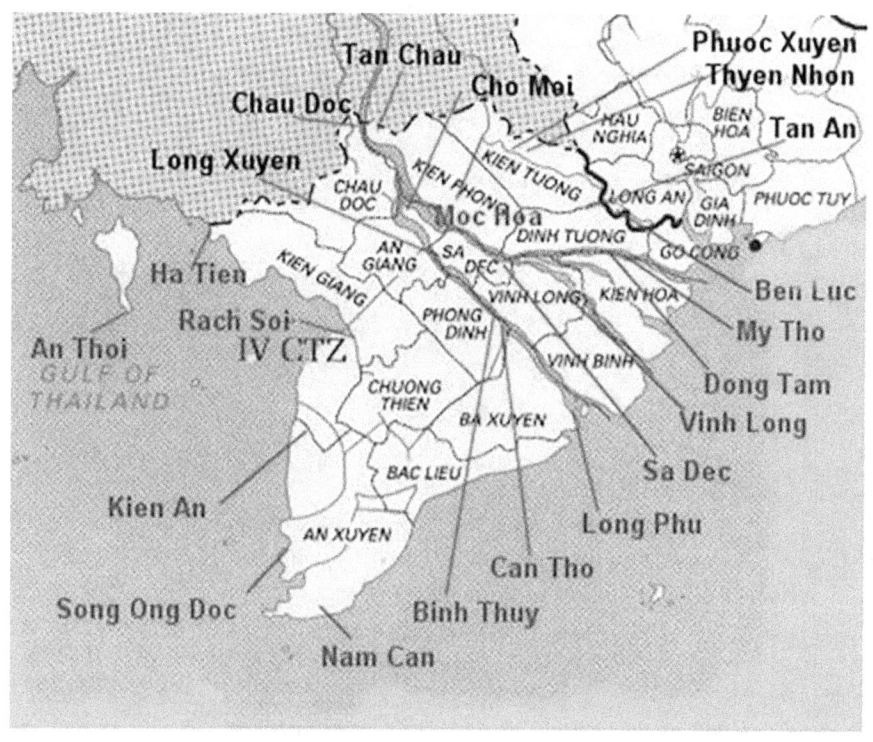

www.ingramcontent.com/pod-product-compliance
Lightning Source LLC
Chambersburg PA
CBHW051518170626
46811CB00002B/881